The male voice came through loud and clear.

'The last thing I need is some husband-hunting female, scarcely out of the schoolroom, who thinks this is going to be some sort of pleasure cruise!'

Lindsey stood feeling the hot colour surge into her cheeks. He was talking about *her*! Taking a deep, controlling breath, she walked indignantly into the room. The speaker broke off, turning to stare at her.

Lindsey stood transfixed, feeling her colour deepen beneath a disturbingly intense appraisal which left her feeling ridiculously shaky. . .

Dear Reader

Love on Call is a very special series by Mills & Boon which perfectly blends romance with the medical profession. You'll read about country vets, flying doctors, general practitioners, midwives and physiotherapists, all finding time for love.

As well as our *Love on Call* novels there are 5 more Mills & Boon series to choose from every month: step back in time with our historical romances *Legacy of Love*, let yourself be seduced by our steamy *Temptation* series, or indulge in a double helping of romance with *Duet*. Enjoy our best-loved *Favourites*, or travel the world with the man of your dreams with our popular Mills & Boon *Romance* series.

A whole variety of heart-warming, racy, or action-packed stories are available every month from Mills & Boon, there's sure to be one for you to enjoy.

The Editor

A DANGEROUS DIAGNOSIS

BY
JEAN EVANS

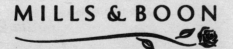

MILLS & BOON LIMITED
ETON HOUSE, 18–24 PARADISE ROAD
RICHMOND, SURREY, TW9 1SR

For Madeleine
with thanks

*First published in Great Britain 1993
by Mills & Boon Limited*

© Jean Evans 1993

*Australian copyright 1993
Philippine copyright 1993
This edition 1993*

ISBN 0 263 78346 4

Set in 10 on 12 pt Linotron Times

*Typeset in Great Britain by Centracet, Cambridge
Made and printed in Great Britain*

CHAPTER ONE

'HI, NEED any help?'

The words coming from behind her sent Lindsey Blake whirling to face the speaker, a slim, dark-haired girl of about her own age, who seemed to be regarding her with some amusement.

'You seem to be lost.'

Lindsey dragged a hand distractedly through her honey-toned hair and gave a rueful grin. 'How did you guess?'

The girl smiled, tanned features emphasising the whiteness of her teeth. 'It's the dazed look. I've seen it before, almost every day, in fact.' She eased the pile of folders she was carrying. 'Perhaps I can help. Where are you trying to get to?'

'Well, I'm supposed to be reporting to the principal medical officer in the ship's hospital.' In a gesture of frustration, Lindsey produced a small hand-drawn diagram. 'I was told it was on deck five.' She turned the piece of paper upside down and shook her head. 'Either someone moved it or I must have got out of the lift on the wrong floor.'

The girl laughed. 'You're on the right deck — you're just on the wrong side of the ship! Don't let it worry you. It happens all the time — you'd be surprised. Even after a three-month world cruise, some of the passengers still never figure it out.'

'I'm beginning to know exactly how they feel,'

Lindsey smiled, 'and I've always rather prided myself on having a pretty good sense of direction.'

'It's easy when you know how. The trick is to follow the coloured signs.' The other girl pointed to the wall. 'Those on the port side of the ship are in red, green signs are starboard. This is port. The hospital is over on starboard. I'm Jill Stewart, by the way.' She stretched out a hand to introduce herself.

Lindsey shook hands. 'Lindsey Blake.'

'Blake?' The girl frowned. 'Blake. . .you're not Dr Blake?' She gave a hoot of laughter. 'We've been expecting you. In fact, we're going to be working together. I'm the senior sister.'

As she returned the firm handclasp Lindsey's smiling gaze for the first time took in the neat, wide-belted white dress, topped by a dark cardigan. 'Of course, I should have realised. . .'

'No reason why you should.' Jill Stewart's grin widened. 'One white dress looks pretty much like another. It's these that make the difference.' She shrugged the cardigan aside to reveal red shoulder epaulettes. 'Only medical staff get to wear these. It's ridiculous, I know, wearing the cardigan, I mean — after all, it is May, but I'm still getting acclimatised. Two weeks ago we were in the Med and the temperatures were in the nineties. Today it's the good old UK and rain, wouldn't you just know it? Look, has anyone actually shown you to your cabin yet?'

Lindsey nodded. 'As soon as I came on board. I decided I'd better dump my bags, literally, and make my presence known. Unfortunately, somewhere along the way I seem to have taken several wrong turns.'

Jill Stewart smiled sympathetically, leading the way

along the carpeted corridor. 'Well, look, I'm on my way over to the hospital now, so I'll take you across. I've just been to see one of our early arrivals in his cabin. We've a party of disabled passengers on board this trip. We usually ask them to arrive ahead of the rest so that we can see them safely settled before the rush starts.'

'You mean it hasn't already?' Lindsey recalled the rapidly growing crowd of passengers in the departure terminal.

The other girl chuckled. 'It's always like this. You'll soon get used to it. We sail at seven this evening, but passengers usually start boarding any time after midday.' She glanced at her watch. 'The important thing is that you made it. I don't mind telling you, with a twenty-four-hour turn-round and a legal obligation to carry a full complement of medical crew, which includes two doctors, there was a certain amount of unrestrained panic to get a replacement in time.'

'Yes, I gather it was all a bit sudden.' Lindsey matched her steps to those of the other girl. 'What happened exactly?'

'You mean they didn't tell you?'

Smiling, Lindsey shook her head. 'I was just told to report.'

'Talk about being thrown in at the deep end!' Jill held a door open. 'As a matter of fact it was all a bit of a shock. Bob Nichols, the chap you're here to replace, had a heart attack the day before we docked.'

'Oh, no!' Lindsey's green eyes clouded. 'Didn't anyone suspect he might have a problem?'

'That's the awful thing, it came out of the blue. No one had any reason to suspect. He'd passed his last medical, otherwise he wouldn't have been on board. You know how rigid the company rules are.'

'Have you heard how he is?'

'Not yet. He was rushed to hospital the minute we docked. We're still waiting for news. Still,' the frown faded, to be replaced by the grin, 'I'd hate you to get the idea that all is doom and gloom. Welcome aboard the *Ocean Empress*, anyway. She's a great ship, and we've got a pretty good medical team, even though I do say so myself. I'm sure you won't have any trouble settling in, once you get to know your way around.'

Lindsey gave a wry grin. 'Red for port, green for starboard.'

'See, I told you it's easy. Come on, we'll cut through here, it's quicker.' They skirted an indoor pool, empty as yet, though a few early arrivals were sitting in the comfortable chairs, enjoying afternoon tea. 'I gather you trained at St Margaret's?' Jill threw Lindsey a look of curiosity and admiration.

'That's right.'

'It was one of the few bits of information we did manage to pick up on the grapevine. I'm impressed.'

Lindsey shot her a wry smile. 'I don't seem to have made a brilliant start so far — getting lost and being late on my first day must be something of a record!'

'Don't worry about it. Give it a couple of days and you'll feel you've been here forever.' They turned a corner as they reached one of the large stairways. 'The hospital is just along here.' Jill caught Lindsey's look of surprise. 'I know, it's so well tucked away, it's easy to see why you might miss it.'

'You can actually get an entire hospital in here?' queried Lindsey.

Jill chuckled. 'It's larger than you might think. We're a completely self-contained unit. We have our own dental surgery, physio department, dispensary, X-ray unit. You mention it, we have it.'

Lindsey unconsciously lengthened her steps. She had a tall, slimly built figure, with long, honey-blonde hair which she had left loose instead of confined in its usual more businesslike French plait, and a face that was gamine rather than classically beautiful, shown in small, straight nose and thickly-lashed, expressive green eyes above a mouth that was generous but firm.

'Through here.' A door swung open beneath the gentle pressure of Jill's hand. 'This is Reception. Passengers wanting to see the duty doctor report and wait here.' She indicated the row of leather chairs. 'And through there is the first consulting-room. Next to that we have the treatment-room, which is where I usually take my morning clinics or carry out minor treatments, and on the other side is the second consulting-room.'

'How many surgeries are there each day?' asked Lindsey.

'Two, morning and afternoon. Both doctors alternate, then there's the crew surgery as well, of course, and any cabin calls.'

'I can see I'm going to be kept fairly busy!'

Jill grinned and glanced at her watch. 'Actually, we may just catch Jim Lewis. With luck he'll probably have finished seeing passengers by now.'

'But we haven't even sailed! People are still boarding.'

'I know,' Jill smiled. 'Jim is actually our radiographer-cum-dispenser. We always get a number of passengers who may be having treatment from their own

GP for a particular condition, in which case they'll bring their own medical notes with them. Some need special diets or specific drugs. It's all information we need to have before we sail. Jim has to deal with any X-rays, lab reports.'

Lindsey frowned. 'Yes, of course. I should have realised.'

'It's like any new job,' Jill added. 'You can't expect to know it all on your first day. You'll feel more at home when I've introduced you to the rest of the team, everyone except Niall anyway.'

'Niall?'

'Dr Grant, our principal medical officer — oh, and he sends his apologies, by the way. He had to attend a meeting of senior officers, but he's looking forward to meeting you. You'll like him. He's a brilliant doctor. He's been with the ship about seven years. Before that he did a stint with the Navy, then a senior registrar's post on shore. We're lucky to have him.'

He was probably quite old, then, Lindsey thought, busily fitting pieces into the mental jigsaw she had been trying to build up of her new boss. Nearing retirement, maybe. 'I'm looking forward to meeting him too,' she said cheerfully. The passengers probably found it quite reassuring to have a fatherly figure as their senior doctor.

Jill Stewart eyed her with a certain degree of amusement as she knocked on one of the doors. 'This is Jim's usual hideout.' Listening, she opened it to greet the sandy-haired man who rose to his feet from behind the desk. 'Hello, are you busy, or can we interrupt? I thought you'd like to meet our new arrival. She'll be taking over from Bob. Dr Blake, Jim Lewis, radiographer. . .'

'And general dogsbody.' Brown eyes twinkled as he came towards Lindsey. He was about forty years old, of medium height, and good-looking. 'So the cavalry has arrived!' One eyebrow rose as he extended his hand in welcome. 'Dr Blake.' His voice bore a heavy trace of Welsh accent. 'And such a nice cavalry too!'

Lindsey laughed as her hand was clasped in a firm, warm grip. 'Mr Lewis.'

'Jim, for heaven's sake. We don't stand too much on formality, not when we're off duty anyway.'

'In that case the name is Lindsey.'

'And very nice too.' He still retained his grasp of her hand. 'So you're going to be our new guardian angel.'

'I've already warned her about you.' Jill's eyes twinkled. 'Just don't take anything he says too seriously,' she advised hardly. 'These Welsh have a way with words. Butter wouldn't melt!'

Jim Lewis grinned. 'Seriously, though, I'm glad you made it. I only wish I had time to stay and talk, but I've got some paperwork to get through right now.' He looked at the clock. 'Perhaps we could meet up later, over coffee. We can usually reckon on a degree of peace and quiet once the passengers go in to dinner.'

'I shall look forward to it,' Lindsey smiled, glancing around the light, airy room with its examination couch, desk, bookshelves and a scattering of potted plants. 'This is lovely.'

'I'll show you the treatment-room later if you like,' Jill said. 'This will probably be your consulting-room.'

'You were right,' said Lindsey, 'this feels more like

home. It could be any on-shore surgery.' The familiarity of it gave her the urge to work.

'I don't suppose you know if Niall is free yet?' Jill moved towards the door.

'Shouldn't think so.' Jim Lewis frowned, gathering up his papers. 'He seemed to think the meeting might go on for a while.'

'Problems?' asked Jill.

He gave a deep-throated laugh. 'Have you ever known a trip when there weren't any? Why should this be the exception?'

Lindsey smiled. 'In that case, it sounds as if the sooner I start work, the better,' she said decisively.

'I can't say we're not glad to see you.' He smiled easily. 'But no one wants to rush you, least of all Niall. If it's any consolation, it does get easier,' he promised. 'Once we get to the sun and people start to relax and unwind. No one wants to be ill. That's the theory, anyway.'

Seeing the smile that didn't quite reach the tired brown eyes, Lindsey shook her head. 'I'd like to feel I'm pulling my weight. That's what I'm here for, after all. Just tell me where and when. I take it Dr Grant has some sort of rota?'

He smiled. 'Tomorrow's soon enough. Niall realises you'll need time to settle in and, barring any unforeseen epidemic, we're not likely to be rushed off our feet, so if you need longer. . .'

'Tomorrow will be just fine,' Lindsey assured him briskly.

'In the meantime, Niall thought you might appreciate a guided tour.' Jill indicated the door. 'I'll do the honours, if you like?'

'I'd love it.' Lindsey was already in hot pursuit.

There were five wards each with ten beds, each sporting matching bedspreads and curtains. 'It may seem a lot for what is, after all, supposed to be a luxury cruise ship,' Jill smiled wryly as they made their way from one ward to the next. 'If it's any comfort, I've never known all the beds to be full, but we have to be prepared for any eventuality. This is the labour ward.'

Lindsey found herself gazing at a fully equipped unit that would have done credit to any major hospital. 'I see you could even carry out a Caesarean delivery,' she remarked.

'So far we haven't had to.' Jill touched wood. 'This is Duncan West, by the way.' She paused to introduce Lindsey to the young man who was checking the various monitors and equipment. 'Duncan is our charge nurse, and this is Helen, Sister Reynolds. If we get any fractious children we always send for Helen. She seems to have a gift for calming them down.'

'I'll remember that,' Lindsey smiled.

'Nice to have you aboard.' The girl returned the handshake. 'Have you worked on ships for long?'

'I'm almost ashamed to admit it, but I'm still something of a beginner.'

'Oh, well, it's all pretty much the same; after all, nursing is nursing wherever you happen to find yourself, don't you think?'

Lindsey wasn't entirely sure she'd agree as they moved on to a gleaming operating theatre. The luxury she had only glimpsed so far was all a far cry from the fading Victorian splendour of St Margaret's with its peeling paintwork and under-staffed, overworked departments. 'I can think of a few consultants, not to mention some very tired registrars,' she added ruefully, 'who'd give their right arm to work in conditions like these.'

'I know what you mean,' said Jill. 'You can't help but be aware of the difference money makes.' She frowned. 'I thought long and hard before I left the NHS to move into the private sector. I felt guilty — after all, they had trained me — but in the end I saw so many of my friends making the move, I saw them working in better conditions, earning so much more for fewer hours,' she grimaced, 'in the end I decided I'd be crazy not to join them.' She slotted a batch of cards into a filing drawer before moving on.

'It's nothing to be ashamed of,' Lindsey said softly. 'What counts is the quality of care we give to the patients.'

'So what persuaded you to leave?'

Lindsey concentrated her gaze on the monitor screen she had flicked into life. 'Several reasons. Long hours. I know,' she gave a slight smile, 'the inevitable cry of most junior doctors.' Her green eyes clouded. 'I felt I needed a new challenge. I saw the shipping company's advertisement and decided to apply. After that everything seemed to happen in a hurry.'

'I know what you mean.'

'You must have specialised in intensive care. Isn't it one of the requirements for a senior sister?' asked Lindsey.

The other girl nodded. 'I did two years on the intensive care unit at my old hospital, as well as the usual casualty and coronary care. This is Niall's particular baby. He set up and worked on a trauma unit before joining the ship. He was actually in on the design and setting up of this hospital when *Ocean Empress* was still in the commissioning stage a few years back. He pushed for most of the equipment you see here.'

Lindsey added the further information to the picture she was still trying to build of the elusive Dr Niall Grant.

'Look, how about a coffee?' asked Jill. 'Or is there anything else you'd like to see right now? Everything's pretty well under control here. We could always go along to the ward-room.'

Lindsey's brow furrowed. 'Actually I'd quite like to stay for a while longer, if you don't mind. I'd like at least to have a picture in my mind's eye of where everything is.' She gave a slight smile. 'To tell you the truth, I hadn't realised quite how much I'd got in the habit of the kind of organised chaos we worked under at St Margaret's. This is going to take a bit of getting used to.'

Jill grinned. 'Take all the time you need. When you've finished, why not pop along and join us? I'll keep the coffee hot and try to save you a biscuit or two. Niall may even have surfaced by the time you join us.'

'I'll be there. By the way, is there somewhere where I can freshen up?'

'Sure, at the end of the ward and along the corridor.'

Fifteen minutes later Lindsey shed her jacket, flicked a comb through her hair and studied her appearance in the mirror.

She was wearing a fashionable knee-length straight skirt, a silk blouse in a vivid jade-green, and slender-heeled shoes. Was the skirt just a shade too short? Even if it was, it was a little late to do anything about it now.

Shrugging, she applied a touch of soft coral lipstick and a dusting of grey-green eyeshadow. A final glance in the mirror and her chin lifted. Why was she worrying so much about what the fuddy-duddy Dr Grant might think of her appearance anyway, when what mattered surely were her professional capabilities, and certainly she had no doubts about those. Her shoes made no sound on the carpeted corridor as she made her way to the wardroom. It wasn't until she had almost reached it that she realised she might have left her watch behind. With a tiny exclamation of annoyance she came to a halt, easing the cuff of her jacket. To her relief the slim gold band encircled her wrist. She must instinctively have replaced it while her mind was on other things.

As she was about to enter the room, the sound of a raised, angry male voice coming from somewhere behind the partially open door caused her to halt in her tracks. What should she do? Make her presence known, or stay where she was and run the risk of being thought an eavesdropper?

As she listened to the unfamiliar male tone, neither option appealed.

'Hell, is this someone's idea of a joke? They know the kind of pressure we have to work under!'

'Oh, come on, Niall,' Jill's voice answered defensively. 'Bob didn't choose to have a heart attack. Maybe it was the pressure that got to him — who knows? Anyway, someone had to take his place. Why not a woman, for heaven's sake?'

A clinking of cups and the sound of running water muffled the rest, but the male voice came through loud and clear.

'The last thing I need is some husband-hunting

female, scarcely out of the schoolroom, who thinks this is going to be some sort of pleasure cruise!'

Lindsey stood feeling the hot colour surge into her cheeks. He was talking about *her*! Her hackles rose. This. . .this man, this total stranger was actually daring to sit in judgement!

Taking a deep, controlling breath, she walked indignantly into the room. The speaker broke off, turning to stare at her as she stood in the doorway.

Lindsey stood transfixed, feeling her colour deepen beneath a disturbingly intense appraisal which left her feeling ridiculously shaky, the ageing, fatherly figure of her imaginings swept away in one fell swoop.

For several seemingly interminable seconds no one moved as the coolly brooding glance subjected her to a flagrantly masculine appraisal.

It was as if an electric current passed through her body. It wasn't just the overwhelming sense of power that seemed to emanate from him as he stood there, it was something in the startlingly blue eyes which raked her slender figure and delicate features with an intensity that almost took her breath away.

She was immediately conscious of every line of the taut muscular body, from his shoulders beneath the open-necked shirt to a slim waist and lean thighs beneath the dark trousers he was wearing.

Her first impression of the man she knew with a sinking feeling could only be Niall Grant was of strong, sun-tanned features which held her gaze as the blue eyes looked coolly into hers, and for the first time in her life her height, which at five feet eight inches had given her an advantage over a lot of men, suddenly seemed diminished. Niall Grant was not a day over thirty-five and aggressively masculine! Behind him she was vaguely aware of Jim Lewis grinning as he uncoiled his tall frame from where he had been half sitting on the edge of the table.

'I think some introductions may be in order,' his Welsh drawl intervened, cutting through the uneasy silence. 'Dr Grant, Dr Blake — Dr Lindsey Blake.' His gaze went from one to the other before he gathered up his cup and papers. 'I think I'll leave you to get acquainted. I'm just about due to cause havoc at a meeting of the passenger Health and Safety Committee anyway.' Winking broadly in Lindsey's direction, he was already heading for the door.

Lindsey swallowed hard, vaguely aware of his stealthy retreat and of Jill, close on his heels, struggling to muffle her laughter. Traitors the pair of them, she thought crossly. They might at least have stayed to offer moral support!

'I'm sorry you had to hear that.' Niall Grant's mouth tightened ominously.

Her head jerked up. Not sorry he had said it, she noted, only sorry she had heard it! Anger tore through her. In any other circumstances she might have found Niall Grant attractive. Right now she resented every bone in his physically perfect body.

'So am I,' she responded bluntly.

His frowning gaze swept over her and there was a glint in the blue eyes that might have been intimidating if she weren't so angry. 'Perhaps if you spent less time lurking behind doors?'

'I was not lurking!' She felt her fury rising. 'I just happened to be in the corridor. I could hardly have expected to hear a complete stranger making such a blatant and. . .and totally unwarranted assassination of my character. Isn't it usual to at least give someone the benefit of a hearing before passing judgement, Dr Grant?' She paused for breath and his laser-blue eyes narrowed, sending tiny ripples of shock running through her as she took in the dark eyebrows, a strong nose and firmly sculpted mouth. She blinked hard, realising that she was staring. Not only that, but he was returning her stare measure for measure.

She felt her colour deepen as his gaze raked her appearance from the top of her honey-blonde hair, lingering over the firm fullness of her breasts and the slender curve of her hips. His left eyebrow rose mockingly

'All right, I take back what I said about the schoolroom. Just how old are you anyway, Dr Blake? You look about nineteen.'

'I'm twenty-six,' Lindsey uttered furiously, her green eyes flashing fire. 'Old enough to have completed my medical training and a year as junior houseman.'

The arrogant mouth twisted. 'And no doubt to have acquired a few personal commitments.'

'What?' For an instant she stared at him, wondering if she had somehow managed to mis-hear.

'It's a straightforward question,' he said. 'I'm asking if there's a boyfriend? Lover?' His gaze narrowed and fell on her left hand. Instinctively she clenched her fingers, but not before she was sure he had seen the white mark etched against her tan.

She drew a deep breath. 'If you have any doubts about my qualifications, Dr Grant. . .'

'Oh, I don't doubt your professional capabilities, Dr

Blake. If they weren't satisfactory, you wouldn't be here.'

'In that case, you know all you need to know.' She faced him, breathing hard. 'The rest is private, strictly off limits.'

The blue eyes narrowed. 'Are you always this defensive?'

'Only when I have to be.' Even in her anger, she found herself having to admit that he was attractive. Attractive and arrogant.

'Your antagonism, Dr Blake,' his voice was ice-cool, 'is it directed at men in general?'

'What antagonism?' she flared.

'I see.' His mouth twisted derisively. 'In that case, it must be directed at me personally. I wonder why?'

She stared at him. 'Do you put all your staff through this kind of third degree, Dr Grant? Or just the females?' she asked tautly.

'Only when I feel it necessary.'

Meaning what? That he obviously imagined she was some kind of flighty, sex-starved man-eater? 'Well, forgive me, Dr Grant, but I am not accustomed to having my personal and professional integrity questioned — and frankly, I resent it.'

He raised a hand to his head in a gesture of weariness. 'Dammit, this isn't personal.'

'It sounds very personal to me,' she snapped. 'Of course, I realise that as far as you're concerned I can't possibly hope to fill my predecessor's shoes, but I do happen to be very good at my job.'

He gave her a steady look. 'Why do I get the feeling that you're deliberately misunderstanding me?' His blue eyes darkened. 'Hell, I was expecting someone. . . more. . .'

'Submissive?' she queried.

His face was set. 'I was about to say more mature.'

'Oh, I'm sure there's every chance I shall age rapidly, Dr Grant,' she snapped. 'And now, if you'll excuse me, I'm sure there must be some work for me to do. Something not too demanding and well within my female capabilities, of course.' Her eyes flashed. 'After all, I'd hate anyone to think I wasn't pulling my weight.' Her hand was already on the doorknob.

'Wait!' He swore savagely, then, as the bleep he was carrying began to sound. 'Dammit. . .we have to talk. . .'

But talking was the last thing she wanted to do, Lindsey decided, as she marched angrily back towards the hospital. Given the chance, what she would most like to do right now was to grab her belongings and plant her feet very firmly back on shore. Except, she realised with a sudden sense of shock, the ship was moving and she hadn't even noticed until now.

Her mouth tightened at the realisation that, like it or not, she and Dr Arrogant Grant were stuck with each other, for the duration of this trip at least.

CHAPTER TWO

LINDSEY was still breathing hard as she strode through hospital reception, with an effort managing to smile at the small group of people sitting there before going through to the consulting-room and flinging her jacket on to the nearest chair.

For a few seconds, as she leaned both hands on the desk to gaze at the unfamiliar surroundings, a feeling of panic hit her. She was committed to this trip, it was too late to do anything about it, but how, she asked herself, was she going to be able to work with a man she didn't even like?

She straightened up, thick lashes veiling her expression as Jill followed her into the room. Right now all that mattered were the patients. Any personal animosity she might feel for Niall Grant must be set aside.

'Are you all right?' Jill closed the door, turning uncertainly to Lindsey.

'What? Oh yes, I'm fine. A little nervous maybe.' Brushing her hair back, she sat at the desk, trying to force her thoughts back into some semblance of order. No one had warned her, back in medical school, that she might have to face outright chauvinism in this day and age. Well, she had news for someone. It was alive and well, and its name was Niall Grant!

She snapped the locks on her briefcase open. 'It looks as if we have a few customers waiting out there,' she managed lightly. 'Give me a couple of minutes, then you can send the first one in.'

Jill frowned. 'Look, you don't have to do this, you know. No one expects. . .'

'I'd rather,' Lindsey explained truthfully. Just now work seemed the best antidote to the frustration that was boiling inside her. Anything to take her mind off the prospect of three weeks spent in enforced close proximity to Niall Grant. She took another steadying breath and reached for the report book. 'Besides, it's what I came here for.'

'Yes, but you haven't even had a chance to unpack.'

'It can wait. Right now I think my number one priority is to prove that I can actually do my job,' Lindsey said tautly.

Jill looked startled at the note of animosity in her friend's voice. 'Look, don't take what Niall said too much to heart. His bark is worse than his bite. I think you just caught him at a bad moment. He's really very nice.'

Lindsey tried to forget the tanned features and dark hair, the arrogant set of jaw. 'I'll have to take your word for that. Obviously I bring out the worst in him.'

Jill gave a wry grin. 'You'll be OK,' she gave the smiling assurance. 'The first day's rough on everyone; tempers get a bit frayed. It's not like being on shore where once the patients are gone you shut up shop and go home. Here we take the patients with us.'

'All the more reason for me to start taking my share of the load as soon as possible.' A smile took the edge off Lindsey's words. 'I take it Dr Nichols and Dr Grant had some sort of work routine?'

'Well, yes. . .'

'May I see it?' Lindsey scanned the rota Jill handed her. Tension had given her a dull, thumping headache so that she absorbed nothing except the first entry on the list. 'I see Dr Nichols would have been due to cover this evening's surgery anyway.'

'He usually took the first surgery, so that Niall could be left free to attend crew briefings.'

'Well, in that case, I see no reason to change things.' Lindsey gave a rueful smile. 'Judging from the looks of the small crowd out there, I'd say there's nothing too urgent. Out of interest, by the way, how many passengers would you usually expect to have on board at any one time?'

Jill grinned. 'On this trip, sixteen hundred, maybe slightly more. On top of that, of course, you have the crew.'

'Sixteen hundred! But that's the same as many practices.'

'Right,' Jill agreed. 'Any patients with potential problems will probably have notes from their GP, advising on any specific treatments or medication they may be taking, and you'll probably get one or two who feel seasick.'

'Seasick?' Lindsey raised an eyebrow. 'We're still in the Solent! In fact, unless you looked out of the window you wouldn't even know the ship was moving.'

'I know.' Jill's grin widened. 'The ship is so well stabilised most people aren't aware of any sensation of movement at all. But I suppose some are more susceptible than others, and there's no reason these days to suffer when a simple injection will cure it.'

'Especially when they've paid to enjoy what, for

some anyway, must be the holiday of a lifetime,'
Lindsey smilingly agreed.

She rose to her feet, reaching for the white coat that
hung on a peg behind the door. There was something
strangely comforting about the metamorphosis it
brought about, even if it was miles too large.

Studying her reflection in the mirror, she grimaced.
'Oh well, at least I look like a doctor! I wouldn't want
to be accused of frightening the patients away.' Besides,
this was her chance to prove that she could cope, the
thought flashed, irritatingly, into her mind. This was
her job. She was good at it, despite what Niall Grant
might think.

'I may need you to show me where things are,' she
turned to Jill, 'but the rest I can manage, even if I have
to bluff my way through.'

The other girl looked up from straightening the
curtains around the examination couch, her brown eyes
clouded. 'About what happened back there. . .what
was said. . .' She chewed at her lower lip. 'I'm sure
Niall didn't mean anything. He's really not like that. . .'

Somehow Lindsey managed to laugh lightly. 'I'm
sure you're right. I was probably far too busy with my
own nerves to take anything in anyway.' The last thing
she needed right now was sympathy, and she certainly
wasn't about to discuss Niall Grant. Other people might
be fooled into thinking he had some redeeming quali-
ties, but she wasn't among that number. Damn the
man! Damn his arrogance!

Sitting at the desk, she drew a deep breath. 'Would
you like to show the first patient in?' She looked
pointedly at her watch, and Jill took the silently offered
cue.

'Just call if there's anything you need and can't find.'

'Will do.' Lindsey reached for her pen and looked up, smiling, as the first patient walked into the room.

She glanced at the brief details on the card Jill handed to her before smiling at the man. 'I see you're diabetic, Mr Allen. How long is it since you were diagnosed?'

'About five years.' Ted Allen was in his early fifties, and slightly overweight. He gave a wry grin. 'It came as a bit of a shock, I can tell you! Collapsed like a pack of cards one day at work and woke up in hospital.' The grin widened. 'Gave the wife a bit of a turn, too.'

'I can imagine it did,' Lindsey smiled. 'I see your condition is diet-controlled rather than by the use of insulin.'

He nodded. 'When they told me what it was, I thought I was going to have to have injections for the rest of my life.'

Lindsey smiled at the still popular misconception. 'You'd be surprised how many diabetics manage to live perfectly normal lives, provided they follow the diet that has been specifically worked out for them, and it *is* important,' she stressed carefully. 'Do you have any problems at the moment?' She frowned at the card. 'I take it you check a urine specimen each morning?'

He shook his head. 'No problems. Our doctor just thought I should let someone know, just in case.'

She nodded, smiling. 'It's a sensible precaution, and you do realise that the ship's catering manager can provide special diets? It's simply a matter of arranging things with the catering staff.' She glanced at the diet sheet contained with the medical records. 'I wonder, do you attend a day centre at all?'

Ted Allen frowned. 'Day centre?'

Lindsey nodded. 'They're becoming very much a part of the treatment of diabetes these days. It might be worth asking your GP if there's one in your area and if so, getting him to refer you.'

'What exactly would be involved?' he asked.

'Well, mainly they offer counselling sessions for people like yourself.' She smiled. 'They can answer all sorts of questions, offer advice on diet. They also encourage patients to take along relatives or friends to participate in the programme.'

He looked a little doubtful. 'How much time would it involve?'

'Probably about an hour for your first visit. They would carry out an initial assessment, based on an evaluation of your lifestyle, age, level of anxiety and so on. Subsequent visits would be shorter, probably about half an hour. But I'm sure it would be time well spent. In the meantime I'll arrange for our dietician to see you and we'll keep a note of this for our own records, but if you're at all worried, do come and see either myself or Dr Grant at any time. We have a twenty-four-hour cover.' Ted Allen left, a satisfied customer, and the next patient walked into the consulting-room.

In the seventh month of pregnancy, Alison Walker needed to be reassured that in the event of her baby's premature arrival, she would be in good hands.

'I'll tell you what we'll do, Mrs Walker——' Lindsey rang the bell summoning Jill '—this is Sister Stewart, our senior nurse. Why don't you hop up on to the examination couch and I'll just take a quick listen to baby's heart and take your blood pressure, then afterwards I'm sure Sister will be only too happy to show you around our labour ward and let you take a look at the facilities we have available. It may help to put your mind at rest.'

'Of course I will,' Jill smiled. 'When is the baby due, Mrs Walker?' she questioned the woman casually.

'Oh, not for another eight weeks yet. But I'd rather be safe than sorry,' she beamed, unaware of the look Jill exchanged with Lindsey. Eight weeks! And they were at sea for three!

With an effort Lindsey managed to keep her expression bland. 'I take it you've been attending your local ante-natal clinic regularly?'

'Oh, yes—well, pretty regularly,' Alison Walker agreed airily. 'It's not so easy without transport and when I was working, of course. But everything was fine last time I went. The doctor said the baby was a nice size and he was in the right position. I told him,' she patted the bulge affectionately, 'as long as he stays put until we're ready.'

Lindsey smiled. 'Well, if you need us, remember that we're here. I can always give you a routine check-up, but obviously, if you get any twinges, even if you think it might just be wind, give us a call. You can dial straight through to the hospital from the phone in your cabin.'

'Don't worry.' Alison Walker struggled to her feet. 'I intend hanging on to junior for a while longer yet, but I'll let you know.'

'Just one more.' Jill handed Lindsey the last file before she led the smiling woman out. 'Mr Baker. His wife is with him, otherwise I don't think he'd be here.'

'You'd better show him in.' Lindsey read swiftly through the notes. The man had a history of chronic bronchitis. She was on her feet when her patient edged his way into the room.

'Do come in, Mr Baker.' She indicated the chair, and smiled what she hoped was a reassuring smile.

He eased himself into it, coughing wheezily as he leaned forward to push a large envelope across the desk. 'My doctor said you'd want these. Been seeing him for years.' He gestured towards the notes Lindsey had taken from the envelope. 'I forgot to renew my prescription before we left home—I didn't think I'd need it.'

Lindsey recognised the medication as one having been proved to be most beneficial in cases like Mr Baker's where it was a matter of offering relief rather than a cure. 'Do you have your inhaler with you?' she asked.

He nodded, tapping his pocket. Lindsey looked at nicotine-stained fingers and said nothing. At Mr Baker's age there was little point and probably less chance of persuading him to change the habits of a lifetime.

Instead, having checked his blood-pressure, she questioned him gently, and said, 'How do you feel now?'

He shrugged. 'Fair enough. I get good days and not so good days.'

Lindsey nodded. 'And what about the medication, does it help?'

'Oh, sure. I'd be in a right state without it.'

'Well, look, I'll write you out a new prescription. If you'd like to pop along to the dispensary, you'll be able to collect your tablets straight away, but if you have any problems, you can always call from your cabin. A doctor is on duty day and night.'

He got to his feet, and she could hear him coughing as he trundled out.

Stretching, she eased her back and began to tidy the desk. All in all it had been a busy but constructive evening's work. Even more, it was gratifying to know that she had coped and coped well, Lindsey thought as she began to clear away.

She had completed her notes when someone tapped at the door and entered. Lindsey frowned, certain that Jill had said there were no more patients, and the frown deepened as she looked up and saw Niall Grant.

Controlling herself with an effort, she rose to her feet, caught completely off guard at the way her pulse raced, totally illogically, at the mere sight of him. It was impossible to distance herself physically in the small room — doing so mentally was the next best thing. She tried to see him objectively, but the results were equally disturbing!

He seemed slightly older than she had first imagined. Thirty-four? Thirty-five, maybe? There were just a few strands of grey in his hair, faint lines around his eyes and the sensuous mouth. *Sensuous*! Lindsey blinked hard. The fact that Niall Grant was a very attractive man was totally irrelevant.

She glanced witheringly in his direction. His earlier comments still rankled, and she said stiffly, 'Can I do anything for you, Doctor? Surgery is over, entirely without mishap, you'll be pleased to hear. I assume that's why you're here, to check up?'

His brows drew into a grim frown and immediately she wished the words unsaid as he dragged a hand wearily across his forehead.

'No, as a matter of fact that isn't why I came. If I'd

had any doubts about your competence you can be sure I wouldn't have left you to cope here.'

Lindsey moistened her suddenly dry lips. 'Oh, well, in that case. . .'

'Hell!' he muttered. 'As a matter of fact, I came to apologise.'

She stared at him uncomprehendingly. 'A-apologise?'

'For dropping you in at the deep end, before you'd had a chance to get your bearings. . .'

'I rather thought that was the object of the exercise.' She looked at him unblinkingly now. 'Well, I hate to disappoint you, Dr Grant, but I haven't lost a single patient so far. Of course, it's early days yet,' she said, unable to resist the gibe. 'I can't say how long I can maintain the odds.'

For a moment, Niall Grant's mouth tightened ominously. 'You sure as hell aren't making this easy, are you?' he said. 'If it's of any interest to you, I scarcely even remember what I said, but if I somehow managed to upset you. . .'

If! Lindsey choked on a retort.

He brushed a hand through his hair, leaving a tuft standing on end. It made him look boyish and oddly vulnerable, and for one crazy moment, she had to stifle an impulse to go to him and smooth it down. She drew herself up sharply. Niall Grant was about as vulnerable as a shark!

'Well, I remember perfectly, and frankly, Dr Grant, I feel nothing but pity for someone who holds such archaic, chauvinistic views in this day and age. You had absolutely no right. . .'

'Not even when it's justified?' He looked at her with slow deliberation, and she felt her breathing deepen.

'What I do with my personal life is nothing whatsoever to do with you.'

'I agree. Provided it doesn't interfere with your work.' His voice was grimly determined, but her own was equally so as she faced him, conscious of the hot colour scorching her cheeks.

'The kind of third degree I was subjected to was *not* justified. You don't know me. You had no reason to suppose that I would allow anyone — or anything — to interfere with my work.'

There was a short silence during which his face clouded before he said, 'You're right, your personal life is none of my business. The things I said may have been unjustified, and the fact that I just happened to be bloody tired and bad-tempered was no excuse. I can only repeat, Dr Blake, I owe you an apology.'

Shock held Lindsey rigid and speechless. At least he had the grace to look shame-faced. The least she could do in return was to meet him halfway. In any case, she told herself, it would be ridiculous to antagonise him, especially as, like it or not, they still had to work together.

'Well, I. . .' She prepared to be magnanimous.

'On the other hand,' he cut in sharply, 'while this may be a pleasure cruise for the passengers, the ultimate responsibility for their welfare and safety is mine. In the event of an emergency we can't simply shunt a patient off to the nearest available cardiac unit or casualty department. We can only rely on each other, and we may as well get one thing straight here and now, Dr Blake. I don't approve of shipboard romances.

I've seen too many end in tears the minute we reach port. A cruise ship is too small a place to allow for lovers' tiffs. I require each member of this team to devote their complete attention to the job in hand. In other words, Dr Blake, I expect one-hundred-per-cent support from every member of this team.'

Her head jerked up. 'And for some reason you doubt my ability to give it?'

'I have no way of knowing,' he responded bluntly. 'Look, we got off to a bad start. My only excuse is that Bob Nichols' heart attack came as a shock. I've known him for years.' He frowned. 'Maybe I should have suspected, seen the signs. . .'

His mouth, a taut line of weariness, relaxed suddenly. 'I've got a great idea. Why don't we call a truce, start again? We have to find a way of working together, and it would be a lot less wearing, don't you think, if we could do so amicably?' Almost as an afterthought he held out his hand.

Lindsey stared at it, shock and surprise still warring within her.

As if he sensed her hesitancy, his gaze softened. 'I don't blame you for what you must be thinking.'

She started, feeling her colour rise at the possibility that he might have an inkling of what was going on in her head at that precise moment!

'It's worth a try, surely?' He sat on the edge of her desk, watching as she tidied it without really thinking about what she was doing. His nearness was making her uneasy, then suddenly his hand came down on hers, halting its movements, sending her gaze flying up to meet his. 'Truce?' he repeated. 'And we can make a start by you calling me Niall. It is my name, you know.'

Incredibly, Lindsey found her defences crumbling. She even managed to smile as she held out her hand.

'All right, Dr. . . Niall. Truce.' Her breath caught in her throat as he stared at her and her pulse-rate accelerated. Someone tapped at the door, and a spasm flickered across his features as she released her breath in a tiny hissing sound.

'Saved by the bell, I think,' he murmured wryly.

She did need rescuing, though not for the reason he imagined. The air was charged with tension coming at her from all directions.

'Oh, Niall,' Jill's voice cut in, 'thank heavens I found you! You're needed urgently on the crew deck. One of the engineers has fallen, and it sounds as if he may have broken his leg. They're not sure about possible internal injuries. I've told them not to attempt to move him until you get there!'

His response was instantly all professional. 'I'll be right there. Find Jim, will you? Warn him I'm going to need some X-rays. Let the duty theatre staff know as well.' He was already striding towards the door, the gentleness of a few moments ago already forgotten, Lindsey realised, with a surprising stab of regret.

'Can I be of help?' she asked.

He paused, frowning, in the doorway. 'You want to?'

She nodded with a sudden feeling of excitement. 'It is what I'm here for.' She needed to earn her place as part of this team, and she realised, with a pounding heart, that she was curious to find out what made this man tick. She faced him and managed to smile. 'Besides, it sounds as if you might be glad of a spare pair of hands, unless. . .unless you'd rather I kept out

of the way, of course?' Her mouth went dry as his gaze
flicked over her, then his mouth curved into a smile.

'What are you waiting for? Let's go!'

What happened next was all something of a blur.
Within seconds, it seemed, the casualty-room was full
of people, all working with a kind of controlled intensity
as everyone swung quietly into action.

'Let's get him over here. Right, get his records. Any
allergies? He's lost a lot of blood. We'll need a cross-
match. Better set up a transfusion.'

Above it all, Niall Grant's voice was calm, decisive —
authoritative, Lindsey thought, as she worked steadily.
Almost without being aware of it she became part of
the team, feeling any initial nervousness slip away as
her actions became automatic and her training took
over.

She scarcely took in the bloody mass that was a face.
There was no time for emotion as the blood was
swabbed away and she concentrated on the badly
gashed cheekbone.

Amazingly she found herself treated to a brief smile
as Niall, hair concealed beneath the operating cap,
glanced briefly in her direction before he bent over the
unconscious man once more. His face was tense with
concentration as he worked to remove tiny splinters of
bone.

'How do things look at your end?' He straightened
up grimly.

'Not as bad as it looked on first assessment. He's
going to need surgery, though.'

'Same here. The thigh is fractured.'

'His BP is falling,' Jill announced quietly.

'Right. Let's get him moved into Theatre.'

It was as if a well-oiled machine sprang into action.

An hour later, Lindsey walked out of the theatre, dragging off her mask and gloves. She wiped the back of her hand across her brow, jumping as Niall spoke quietly from behind her.

'Well done!' His hand rested briefly on her shoulder and she felt the colour surge into her cheeks. Then he was gone.

As she watched the door swing gently to a close behind him, Lindsey was left with the crazy feeling that she must have imagined those few seconds when something, even if she couldn't put a name to it, had passed between them.

Suddenly weary, she raked a hand through her hair, lifting its weight from her neck. It had been a long and eventful day. A while ago she had felt hungry; now her appetite seemed suddenly to have faded. Having tidied her desk, she looked round the small room before snapping off the light. Maybe she would skip dinner and simply go to her cabin, unpack her things and get an early night.

Something told her she was going to need all the energy she had, working with Niall Grant for the next three weeks.

With the last of her dresses hanging in the wardrobe, undies neatly folded in the drawer, Lindsey switched on the radio and bedside lamp.

The cabin was surprisingly spacious, even if it did lack the little human touches that made it a home. But then it was only going to be for a matter of weeks, so what did it matter anyway?

She sighed. Her contract with the company was

temporary, allowing her to cover for the emergency created by Bob Nichols' illness. When she got back she would have to renegotiate it, settle to a different ship.

A tiny frown of annoyance tugged briefly at her brow. Things hadn't worked out quite the way she had imagined. The very reason she had applied to the shipping company for a job was that she felt she needed a complete break, a change of scene. Not so much to get over the final break-up of her relationship with Paul—that had been inevitable, she realised that now. In fact, looking back, she sometimes wondered how it had lasted as long as it did.

She couldn't really even remember when it had started. Perhaps that was partly the trouble. They had met in medical school, where Paul Forrest was a year ahead of her. They had more or less drifted into a relationship, meeting at lectures, having the occasional meal together.

Paul had been good company. They had a lot in common, mostly work, Lindsey acknowledged with a rueful grimace now. Training to be a doctor hadn't left too much time for socialising, and maybe that was another reason why she hadn't suspected that Paul was one of those rare people dogged by obsessive jealousy.

It had started so insidiously, the odd remark if she happened to meet a friend when they were together. At first she had even felt vaguely flattered that he should feel jealous, as if, in some way, it was a kind of measure of the way he cared.

It was only later, after they had become engaged, that he had seemed to change, so slowly at first that she was scarcely even aware of it happening until, one day at a party given by a fellow student, someone, she couldn't even remember who, had planted a playful kiss on her cheek. That was all it was, a meaningless kiss, but Paul had stormed out, leaving her to follow, making excuses as she left, conscious of her friends' sympathetic glances, telling herself they didn't understand. Paul was highly strung, working too hard. But weren't they all. . .?

It had been Christmas when she finally knew she had to call an end to it, before the relationship destroyed her completely. On Christmas Eve, listening to herself making yet more excuses on the telephone, explaining why they couldn't make it to a family party, hearing her sister's disappointment. 'But we hardly see you at all these days. Is it something we've done? Honestly, Lindsey, you can't be working all the time. . .'

In one blinding flash then, she had realised how much she had actually given up for Paul in a futile attempt to avert his jealous outbursts—friends, family, social life, even smiling. . . And the irony was that he had been shocked when she had handed him back his ring.

No, Lindsey told herself, as she showered and slipped into a warm towelling robe, it had actually been over for a long time. She simply hadn't wanted to admit it.

Emerging from the shower ten minutes later, skin glowing and towelling her damp hair, she was galled to discover that she was no longer tired and, worse, that her stomach was actually rumbling with hunger.

She stared at her watch. Nine o'clock, a little late to get dressed and go in search of food, especially when she wasn't in the mood to be sociable.

Suddenly she remembered that she had a bar of chocolate somewhere.

She was hunting through her bag when someone

tapped at the door. With an exclamation of frustration she went to open it, gave a violent start and swallowed hard.

Niall Grant stood there, only now, instead of a uniform, he was wearing an expensively tailored dark suit and a smile that sent a very odd tremor sliding down her spine.

Lindsey stared at him, speechless.

One dark eyebrow rose fractionally. 'I've come to take you to dinner,' he announced calmly.

CHAPTER THREE

'I TAKE it you haven't eaten?'

For a second Lindsey stood unmoving as Niall's gaze swept with slow appreciation over her body, taking in every curve which, she realised, blushing hotly, must be emphasised beneath the damp robe. Involuntarily she pulled it more securely around her in a jerky movement, her flush deepening as his mouth curved with mocking laughter.

'Actually, I'm not very hungry.' She voiced the lie without even understanding the logic behind it. There *was* no logic, except that this man's presence seemed to have an uncannily disturbing effect on her nerves.

Without her even being aware of it he had somehow moved into the cabin, leaving her standing at the open door. She swallowed the sudden tightness in her throat.

'As a matter of fact, I thought I'd have an early night.'

'At nine o'clock?' His half-smile was gently mocking.

'It's been a very long day, and I still have to finish unpacking,' she prevaricated.

'You also have to eat,' he pointed out reasonably, 'and since I feel responsible for your having missed lunch, not to mention tea, I insist.'

Lindsey threw him a sharp look before her gaze fell. Why did she get the feeling that in any argument with Niall Grant, he would always come out the winner? 'Isn't it a little late?'

40

'This is a ship,' he said evenly. 'Food is available twenty-four hours a day, for those who want it.'

'But then we aren't passengers,' she couldn't resist throwing his own reminder at him.

The blue eyes narrowed. 'True. On the other hand, even the crew must eat. It may have escaped your notice, Dr Blake, but you weren't the only one who missed dinner and, frankly, I'm starving, so why don't you stop arguing and go and get dressed? It will save a lot of time.'

If it hadn't been for the fact that her stomach chose that precise moment to rumble loudly she might still have argued. In the normal course of events, she decided, there was no way she would *choose* to eat with this man. As it was, she was very much aware of the healthy return of her appetite, so why cut her nose off to spite her stomach?

'Give me fifteen minutes,' she said.

'Make it ten,' he told her, in a voice which brooked no argument.

She made it with thirty seconds to spare.

'Bring a jacket,' Niall told her quietly. 'It can get chilly up on deck.'

She ate ravenously, suddenly even more hungry than she had imagined. When she finally put her dessert spoon down on the empty plate, it was disconcerting to look up and see Niall watching her, a glint of amusement in his eyes.

'For someone who wasn't hungry, I'd say you did pretty well!'

She blushed guiltily as she realised he had refused a sweet, opting just for coffee, but then, she doubted that anything could test his willpower and not lose. 'It must be the sea air. I definitely mustn't make a habit of this, or none of my clothes will fit. Don't they say it's possible to gain half a stone on a three-week cruise?'

Blue eyes met hers. 'They do, but I don't think you need to worry. There's nothing wrong with your figure.'

The genuine note of admiration in his voice sent a tiny and thoroughly illogical *frisson* of pleasure running through her, and she felt the faint tide of colour swim into her face as she sent him an answering smile. 'Not yet, maybe, but there soon would be. The food is marvellous!'

'What did you expect?' A faint smile twisted the corners of his mouth. 'Dry biscuits and water?'

Lindsey relaxed, feeling she was somehow on safer ground. 'Well, not exactly.'

'A happy crew make a happy ship.' Niall drained his glass and looked at his watch. 'Would you like more coffee?' She shook her head. 'In that case, shall we take a brief walk up on deck? I don't suppose you've had a chance to see anything yet.'

'Won't it be too dark to see anything now?' she queried.

He smiled. 'You'd be surprised how much traffic there is out there. Besides, you'll probably still be able to see the lights from the shore.' So near yet so far, the thought tumbled into her mind. 'Don't forget your jacket.'

She rose to her feet, and had half turned when her bag fell to the floor, scattering its contents in all directions. Annoyed with her own clumsiness, she bent to retrieve it, just as he followed suit. Their bodies collided and, momentarily winded, she rocked backwards. Instinctively Niall reached out, grasping her arms, drawing her towards him as he straightened up.

'Here, let me.' In one fluid movement, he swept up the bag and its contents, placing it in her hands.

Lindsey felt the breath catch in her throat as a feeling of physical awareness swept through her, then she moved out of his grasp.

'Thanks,' she muttered.

'Think nothing of it.' His eyes narrowed briefly, then he draped the jacket round her shoulders before leading the way to the stairs.

Lindsey gasped as she stepped on to the deck and was hit by a wave of cold air. 'You're right, it's freezing out here!'

His hand under her arm steadied her as they moved to stand at the rail. 'It seems worse than it is. It's the movement of the ship. She picks up speed in the late evening, after most of the passengers have eaten. She covers the greatest distance at night while they're all asleep. The day after tomorrow they'll wake up to find themselves in Madeira.'

Lindsey leaned against the rail, conscious of his nearness, her mouth dry with a nervousness that seemed to have no logic to it. He was right, she thought, gazing into the distance, there were lights everywhere, some from passing ships and others which could only be the shoreline.

'I've read about the island of Madeira, but I've never been there. It sounds wonderful. Do you. . . I mean, is there time to go ashore?'

'I try to make time. Some places obviously hold more attraction than others.'

'You must enjoy the life?' Pushing an errant strand

of hair from her eyes, she turned to look at him, and found him watching her.

'It has its moments,' he said softly.

Suddenly she was having difficulty swallowing. With a sense of shock, it occurred to her that Niall might be married. She shivered slightly, and as if instantly aware of it, he straightened up.

'It's getting late. I'll see you back to your cabin.'

Suddenly, frustratingly, Lindsey found that all trace of her former tiredness had vanished. Maybe it was the fresh air, but now she felt thoroughly wide awake, and the last thing she wanted was to sleep.

Outside the door he paused long enough for her to fit the key into the lock.

'Well, goodnight, then, Dr Grant.' Her voice sounded husky.

He gazed down at her for a long moment, studying her features as if trying to re-gather his thoughts. His mouth tightened, a nerve pulsing in his jaw as, almost reluctantly, his hand brushed against her cheek as he eased her jacket more securely round her shoulders, then he pushed her gently away. 'Goodnight, Lindsey.'

At least that was what she thought he said, but she couldn't be absolutely sure as he turned on his heel and walked away, leaving her standing in the darkness of her cabin.

The sound of the telephone shrilling by the side of her bed brought her gasping back to wakefulness.

Lindsey lay for a few seconds, battling with a sense of disorientation, one arm flung over her face as she tried to remember where she was.

Groaning, she reached for the light switch. Who on

earth could that be at this hour? Dragging a hand through her hair, she reached for the phone. 'H-hello?'

There was a moment's hesitation before a deep male voice spoke in her ear. 'Niall here — Niall Grant. I hope I didn't disturb you?'

More than he could possibly know, she thought wildly, staring at the alarm clock in disbelief. In spite of falling into bed feeling wide awake and convinced she would be awake for hours, she must have fallen into a deep sleep that had lasted for all of ten minutes!

'No — ' she cleared her throat ' — not at all.' Instinctively her hand drew the sheet higher before she chided herself for the gesture. It wasn't as if he could see her in the flimsy satin nightdress, was it?

His voice sounded a little strained. 'I've been working on a report and I've only just realised how late it is. You were probably asleep.'

'As a matter of fact I was just finishing unpacking.' She crossed her fingers on the lie.

'In that case, I'm glad I caught you. I forgot to mention earlier that I'll be standing in for emergency cover tonight.'

Lindsey closed her eyes on the shocking realisation that she hadn't even given it a thought! 'That's very good of you, but there's really no need. I can cope. . .'

'I'm sure you can,' came the quiet rejoinder. 'In fact, I would have been due to cover tonight anyway, but it occurred to me that you might be worried. I wasn't attempting to question your capabilities. I think I've already learned my lesson on that particular score.'

There was a hint of laughter in his voice, and in spite of herself, Lindsey gave a rueful grin. 'I may as well confess, I hadn't given it a single thought.'

They both laughed, then there was an awkward silence.

'Yes, well, in that case you can go to bed and sleep easy.'

Fat chance of that, Lindsey thought. 'I'll have got my bearings by tomorrow, so you won't need to stand in for me,' she said, 'but tonight, I don't mind admitting, I'll be glad to catch up on some beauty sleep. It's been quite a day.' In more ways than one!

'I hadn't noticed that you need it.' There was a moment's pause before his voice came back with added briskness. 'So I'll cover tonight, then, and perhaps you'll take the early passenger surgery.'

'I'll be happy to. . .'

But the receiver had already clicked into place and she knew he hadn't even heard.

In fact, she didn't see him at all when she made her way to the hospital the following morning.

A brief foray on to the upper deck, and Lindsey had retreated back into the warmth. The ship was moving more slowly, but a blustery breeze and flying spray had discouraged all but the very hardy from taking an early morning stroll.

Even so, she had lingered long enough to watch a tanker ploughing a parallel course, though in the opposite direction, probably bound for the big oil refinery. She had been surprised, in fact, to discover just how many other vessels there were out there, and would have liked to stay longer, but duty called.

Sally Morrisey, the night sister, had just completed the hand-over as Lindsey walked into Reception. She nodded, smiling ruefully, in the direction of the waiting area. 'It looks as if you're in for a busy morning. It's pretty full out there.'

'Not so very different from general practice, is it?' It was Jill who, smiling, handed Lindsey a batch of cards. 'Want me to bring in some coffee later?' She popped a pen into the pocket of her white dress.

'Great idea!' Lindsey grinned, already heading for the door. 'I'd better get started. Give me a couple of minutes.'

'Will do.'

Lindsey dropped the cards on to the desk, took a deep breath and checked her appearance in the mirror, seeing the fashionable dark tailored skirt and the short-sleeved blouse with its red epaulettes. She decided purposely against the white coat. Passengers were on holiday; they didn't want to be reminded too much of illness or its associated formalities.

She seated herself at the desk, relocated a floral display and smiled as the first patient walked into the room.

All in all she worked solidly for two hours, and it was a relief when she was finally free to take an official coffee break.

Wandering into the wardroom, she found Jim Lewis helping himself to coffee and Jill already seated, glancing through a magazine.

'We were just wondering whether we should send out a search party,' they told her.

Lindsey laughed. 'Don't worry, there's no danger of me getting lost this time. I smelled the coffee and followed my nose. Mm, I'm ready for this!'

'I know the feeling.' Jim handed her a cup. 'Talking of which, I'd better get back. I've got a couple of lab reports to rush through for Niall.'

'Not drumming up custom for us, I hope?'

'Blame the boss.' He grabbed another biscuit from the plate before handing it to Lindsey. 'Anyway, why should some of us do all the work?' He was gone, grinning as a magazine flew through the air, missing him by inches as the door closed.

Lindsey sank into a chair, easing off her shoes.

'How did it go?' asked Jill.

'Actually it wasn't too bad.' Lindsey leaned back, relishing the hot coffee. 'No worse than my first day as a medical student, anyway. I seem to recall that that was just about my worst nightmare — trailing around after a consultant who thought medical students were the lowest form of life — which they were, of course.'

'They say it gets easier,' Jill grinned. 'Mind you, they never actually say when, and you did rather get dropped in at the deep end. You'll have to take my word for it, we don't get that kind of trauma too often.'

'I'm relieved to hear it.' Lindsey relaxed, smiling, then sobered to ask, 'How is the patient, by the way? I haven't had a chance to see him yet this morning.'

'He's doing nicely. Niall took a look at him first thing, when he did a ward round. Obviously it's going to take time, but he'll be fine.'

'Oh, I'm glad.'

Jill poured another cup of coffee. 'That was quite a job you did on him, you and Niall between you.'

Lindsey spooned sugar into her own cup. 'I don't think I had a great deal to do with it.' She gave a wry smile. 'To tell you the truth, I felt all fingers and thumbs. I was terrified, even though I wasn't operating. It was far worse than my first day on the wards.'

'For heaven's sake, why? Niall was impressed.' Jill

shot a glance in Lindsey's direction and smiled. 'I told you, Niall's not the tyrant you seem to take him for.'

Lindsey swallowed a mouthful of too-hot coffee, feeling it burn her throat as the cup rattled into the saucer. 'Yes, well, I think I'll reserve judgement, if you don't mind.'

'Chicken!' Jill grinned, and was handing her empty cup to Lindsey when the door opened and Niall walked in, a harassed expression marring his attractive features. 'Talk of the devil, my exit cue, I think,' muttered Jill, making her excuses and slipping away.

'I seem to spend most of my time at meetings these days.' There was a taut edge to Niall's voice. 'I should have been an accountant or an administrator instead of a doctor! If you're doing the honours, I'll have mine black, two sugars.'

A small pulse began to hammer at the base of Lindsey's throat as she rose to her feet to pour more coffee. 'I know what you mean,' she murmured, willing her hands to remain steady as she handed him the cup. As he took it their fingers met, invoking so vivid a memory of the few seconds she had spent in his arms that she jerked away, spilling coffee into the saucer.

He was wearing dark trousers and a white, short-sleeved shirt. She found herself gazing with fascination at his hair, which curled slightly against his collar, before her gaze rose to meet the full impact of his startlingly blue gaze.

'Sleep well?' he asked.

'Fine, thanks.' She took several deep breaths, hoping he would put the sudden bright colour in her cheeks down to the hot coffee she had just swallowed. 'How's the injured crew member this morning?'

'Not too happy.' He stifled a yawn. 'God knows how he managed to fall downstairs. I've started an investigation. The Health and Safety people will need a full report. Perhaps you'd take a look at him later?'

'Yes, of course. I'll be doing a round this afternoon.' She frowned. 'Are you worried about him? I mean, I thought he was doing pretty well.'

'He is, in so far as recovery from the operation is concerned.' Niall frowned. 'That was a pretty nasty injury. We did what we could but, ideally, I'd like to see him moved to a proper unit, specialising in orthopaedics. He's going to need intensive physiotherapy.'

'Is there anything you can do?' she asked.

'If I feel the situation warrants it, I can arrange to get him lifted off by helicopter and flown to the nearest civilian hospital. Obviously, certain things have to be taken into consideration — the patient's condition, distance.' His dark brows furrowed. 'I'll see how it goes. By the way, has anyone explained the emergency code to you?'

Lindsey half turned. 'No, they haven't.'

He was stirring more sugar into his cup. 'It's pretty much like the procedure at any hospital when an emergency crops up, except that here we tend to use a little more subtlety. After all, we don't want to put the passengers off their lobster Thermidor, do we?' He smiled, and the effect was devastating!

'No, I suppose not.'

'We use the word "sundowner". If you hear it over the tannoy, you'll know we probably have a cardiac arrest. The message will also give you the location of the incident.'

Lindsey nodded. 'I'll remember.' She was on the

point of leaving again when Jim Lewis erupted back into the room. Smiling, she wondered whether he ever moved at a normal pace.

'Niall,' he said cheerily, 'those reports you wanted— I've left them on your desk along with the X-ray plates. You were right, there is a fracture. I don't envy you having to tell the dear lady that she'll have to spend the rest of her holiday with her wrist in plaster!'

On the other hand, Lindsey found herself thinking, if Niall smiled at her the way he had smiled a few minutes ago, the dear lady probably wouldn't even need an anaesthetic!

Suddenly becoming aware of his blue gaze being levelled in her direction, she turned a smile into a cough, and promptly spilled coffee into the saucer.

'Damn!' She leapt to her feet mopping furiously at the small wet patch on her skirt. That would teach her to keep her mind off other things!

Jim came unwittingly to her aid, stepping forward to take the cup. 'By the way, if Cinderella would like an escort to the ball tonight, I'm ready and waiting, and promise faithfully not to turn into a rat at the stroke of midnight.'

Lindsey grinned—she couldn't help it. Jim Lewis was an outrageous flirt, but since he made no bones about it, she knew it was quite harmless.

'Ball?' she queried.

'Second night at sea, the captain always holds a formal reception. It's an opportunity for the passengers to meet members of the crew. Everyone gets to wear their best bib and tucker.'

Without turning her head, Lindsey could feel the

weight of Niall Grant's blue eyes watching her, a frown suddenly darkening his gaze.

'Well, I. . .' she began.

'Aren't you supposed to be on call this evening, Dr Blake?' The set of his mouth suggested that he was angry, and Lindsey felt the dull colour rising in her cheeks as she wondered why. Then it suddenly hit her that, of course, he didn't approve of relationships. But surely he couldn't think. . .?

She managed to keep her own voice even as she smiled sympathetically at Jim. 'Yes, of course. How silly of me to have forgotten!'

'That's no problem,' he grinned, unabashed. 'We have a perfectly efficient paging system, isn't that right, Niall?'

Lindsey saw the dark brow come down and from his thunderous expression could tell Niall was furious. On the other hand, a spark of rebellion asserted itself. Just because he was her boss, that didn't give him the right to organise her social life as well!

She flashed him a look before bestowing her nicest smile on Jim. 'In that case, I shall look forward to it.'

The firm set of Niall Grant's mouth suggested that she was treading on dangerous ground. 'Just remember,' he shot a look in her direction as he set aside his half-empty cup and strode towards the door, 'that we're supposed to be on parade, Dr Blake, not enjoying ourselves.'

Perish the thought! 'Yes, sir,' she returned shortly, just as the door slammed to a close, rocking on its hinges.

CHAPTER FOUR

LINDSEY slid the X-ray on to the screen, leaning forward to study it more closely. With a finger she traced a thin white line. 'Mm—well, there does appear to be something there.' She frowned. 'Let's have the bright light closer. Yes—there, look, a hairline, but I couldn't say with absolute certainty that it's a fracture.'

Jill straightened up. 'Shall we go ahead and plaster, then?'

'Yes, I'm afraid so.' Smiling ruefully, Lindsey handed the plate back. 'We'll treat it as a scaphoid fracture. Plaster and re-X-ray in ten days. In the meantime, I'll prescribe some painkillers. It's all we can do.'

Jill slid the film into a large envelope. 'What rotten luck it had to happen now! Still, I suppose it could have been worse. It could have been her leg. Not that that's much comfort.'

'I'll have a word with her if you send her along, once the plastering's taken care of,' Lindsey straightened up from writing a brief note, kneading the muscles at the back of her neck in an attempt to relieve some of the tension. 'I take it we've had a couple of admissions?'

'Right.' Jill reached for the report book. 'One member of crew, one passenger. This is the crew file. Andrew Clarke, aged thirty-five.'

'I gather Dr Grant saw him immediately following the accident.' Lindsey scanned the report and raised one eyebrow. 'Spiral fracture of the tibia. We don't see too many of those.'

'That's what I told Mr Clarke.' Jill grinned. 'I got the feeling he wasn't too impressed.'

Lindsey chuckled. 'Perhaps we can cheer him up with the news that he'll only be on the ward for a couple of days. You said there was a passenger?'

'Yes, that's right.' Jill frowned. 'I'm slightly worried about Mr Deakin. Niall got a cabin call and went to see him during the night. Mr Deakin was complaining of breathlessness. Apparently he has a history of COADs—chronic obstructive airways disease. Niall spent some time with him, making him more comfortable and generally trying to reassure him.'

So that explained the display of bad temper. Lindsey experienced a sharp pang of guilt. He couldn't have had more than a couple of hours' sleep.

'Any chest pain?' she queried briskly.

'Apparently not, otherwise Niall would have insisted on him being admitted. As it was, he decided not to push it, but Mr Deakin came down about an hour ago. These are the details we have so far—oh, plus a letter from his own GP.'

'Obviously his doctor must have anticipated something like this.' Lindsey read through the report. 'He's taking the recognised medication.' She glanced at Jill. 'He *has* been taking it?'

'Apparently. It was the first thing I asked.'

Lindsey nodded. 'Well, it's a recognised symptom of the condition that an attack can come out of the blue. Let's go and have a chat with him and see if we can put his mind at rest.'

Jill followed her to the ward where Mr Deakin was

sitting in a chair beside the bed. He looked pale and distressed.

'Hello, Mr Deakin. I'm Dr Blake. I hear you're not feeling too well.' Lindsey sat on the bed. 'If I could just listen to your chest, get some idea of what's going on in there?'

Mr Deakin smiled wanly. 'You go ahead, Doc. I'm used to it.'

Straightening up a few minutes later, Lindsey nodded and smiled reassuringly. 'Well, I don't think it's anything too drastic. You've got a bit of an infection bubbling away in there, but we'll prescribe something that should clear it up fairly quickly. In the meantime, you should continue taking your other medication and we'll see if we can ease the breathing for you. With luck you'll be able to carry on and enjoy your holiday.'

His eyes brightened visibly. 'I'm grateful, Doctor, and I know the wife will be pleased too.'

'That's what we're here for.'

Lindsey slipped the stethoscope into the pocket of her white coat as they headed back to reception. 'He'll be fine,' she said. 'We'll keep him in for observation just for tonight. That way we can keep an eye on him and he'll feel reassured. I'll write him up for that medication now.'

'And all being well there's no reason why he shouldn't go ashore tomorrow morning.'

'Ashore?' Lindsey ran a hand through her hair. 'Of course, I'd forgotten — we'll be in Madeira.'

'Hadn't you noticed the weather gradually improving?' Jill laughed. 'You just watch. Everyone will be down for early breakfast. By nine-thirty they'll have collected their boarding passes and by ten the ship will be virtually deserted.'

'Are you going ashore?' asked Lindsey.

'I'm not sure yet.' Smiling, Jill rearranged packets of sterile dressings. 'I haven't had a chance to ask if Tony's managed to get any time off.' Tony was Jill's boyfriend, Lindsey had learned — one of the crew members.

'I expect you've seen it all before.' Lindsey sighed enviously. 'I dare say the novelty must wear off after a time.'

'Believe me, Madeira is always worth seeing again,' said Jill. 'It's one of the most beautiful islands I've ever seen. Exotic flowers grow wild. The whole island is like one huge tropical greenhouse, with the added attraction that it never gets too hot — a nice steady seventy degrees.' She looked up, smiling. 'If you get the chance to go ashore, take it. It must be the nearest thing to the Garden of Eden!'

But the trouble with the Garden of Eden, Lindsey found herself thinking, was that it had some rather disturbing connotations, not to mention the odd serpent!

She drew a steadying breath, glancing at her watch. 'The crew member who underwent surgery. . . Peter Bates, wasn't it? He fell down the stairs.'

'That's right. He seems brighter this morning.'

'Yes, I thought so too. On the other hand, it was a pretty bad injury.' Lindsey flipped a page in the notes. 'We did what we could surgically, but Niall's right, it needs specialist orthopaedic attention. I had a chat with him earlier. I gather he's a keen footballer.'

'Oh dear!'

'Precisely.' Lindsey smiled wryly. 'It's not just his job

that's at stake, though goodness knows that's important enough; it's his way of life.'

'So what will you do?' asked Jill.

'Recommend that he's taken ashore at the next port of call and arrange for him to be flown home to an orthopaedic unit. I'll have another chat to Niall and set everything up. I'll give you the word as soon as we have a flight.'

'Fine. We'll have everything ready this end.'

Lindsey closed the notes. 'Didn't you mention that someone had asked to see me?'

'Oh yes, a Mr and Mrs Hammond,' said Jill. 'They asked for an appointment, so I arranged it for this afternoon. I gather it's in connection with Mrs Hammond's condition. They didn't go into details, but apparently they have medical records from their own GP and a letter from their local hospital.'

'Right, in that case I'll see them now.' Lindsey hesitated. 'Is the reception office empty?'

'Sure, the last patient left a while ago.'

'I'll see them in there, then. It's less formal than the consulting-room.' Lindsey made her way to the office, taking a few seconds to run a comb through her hair before the door opened and the Hammonds came hesitantly into the room.

'Mr and Mrs Hammond?' She smiled. 'Take a seat, and tell me what I can do to help.'

There was a momentary pause during which Steve Hammond glanced at his wife. He was in his late thirties; his wife, Anne, according to her case notes, was three years younger, and looked more.

Short, fashionably cut brown hair only seemed to give added emphasis to her thin features, deepening the shadows beneath her eyes. She sat holding her husband's hand and gave a brief nod as if in answer to his unspoken question, then when he cleared his throat awkwardly she patted his hand and spoke for him.

'The thing is, Doctor, I've been having treatment from my GP for some time now. Eighteen months, in fact, as well as making regular visits to my local hospital, and they felt that. . .well, in the circumstances, my being away from home, I should bring my notes and this letter with me.' She fumbled in her bag, handing an envelope to Lindsey. 'Dr Simpson explains everything.'

'It's all there, Doctor.' Steve Hammond seemed to find his voice at last, but behind his smile, Lindsey couldn't help but catch a faint note of desperation.

'It's just that. . .well, you see. . .'

'I'm dying, Doctor,' Anne Hammond put in quietly, and miraculously somehow even managed to smile. 'Oh, it's all right,' as she registered the look of shock in Lindsey's eyes, 'I've known for quite some time. From the beginning, since they took the blood tests. I'd already begun to realise something was wrong, but then they confirmed it. It's my bone marrow, you see. . .'

'She needs a transplant.' Steve Hammond passed his tongue over his lips. 'We've tried for a donor. . .'

'You haven't been able to find a suitable match,' Lindsey put in quietly.

His wife nodded. 'We've had time to adjust to the idea.'

The flicker of anguish in the man's eyes made Lindsey wonder if that was entirely true, for him at least, but she found herself marvelling that this tiny woman could appear so calm.

Her gaze went from Anne Hammond's fragile, pale face to the records spread out on her desk, and she felt her stomach contract. X-rays, blood tests, dates of emergency hospital admissions, visits to the general practitioner, medication. It was, as Steve Hammond said, all there, but there was nothing, she realised, in all those pages to tell her of the particular hell this couple must have been through.

She swallowed hard. 'I see from your notes that your doctor saw you a few days ago.' Her gaze went to the letter. 'Are you experiencing any worsening of the symptoms? If so, I can. . .'

'Oh, no, we don't want you to do anything,' the woman put in softly. 'We don't want to be any trouble. I have my tablets. It's just that — well, you see. . .'

'Some days are not so good,' Mr Hammond put in quietly. 'She gets very tired.' Lindsey noticed the involuntary tightening of his hand over his wife's. 'We thought you should know, in case. . .'

'We don't know how much time there is, you see.'

As if it was the most ordinary thing in the world, Lindsey found herself thinking. Of course, she had come up against death, or the prospect of it, many times in the course of her work, but somehow she had never acquired the sort of immunity against emotional involvement, that almost instinctive shutting off, as so many of her colleagues had seemed to do.

She felt her throat tighten. 'Mrs Hammond, forgive me, but. . .did you, both of you, give serious thought to the possibilities of what might happen when you decided to come on a cruise?'

'Oh, yes.' They smiled at each other. 'We thought about it for quite some time.'

Steve Hammond frowned. 'I was against it at first. I thought it would be too tiring—for Anne, that is.'

Looking at his wife's pale features, Lindsey could understand his concern.

'I understand the risks,' his wife said quietly. 'I know there may be days when I feel too tired, but you see, I decided. . .we *both* decided that this was what we wanted to do. It's always been a dream of ours, to come on a cruise.' She smiled. 'We couldn't afford it for our honeymoon, but we always promised ourselves, half jokingly, that one day. . .' She broke off, lowering her gaze fractionally for an instant before looking directly into Lindsey's eyes. 'I want Steve to have something good to remember, and I'd like to fulfil my own dream before it's too late. Not many people get the chance to do that, do they?'

Lindsey swallowed hard in an effort to find her voice. 'No, they don't.'

The Hammonds were on their feet. She rose, following them to the door. 'If you need me, no matter what time of day or night, just call.'

'We will,' Mr Hammond gave the assurance. 'We're going ashore tomorrow.'

'You have your medication?' asked Lindsey.

They both nodded, and seconds later the door closed behind them.

Lindsey sat at her desk, willing her breathing back to normal. Anne Hammond's courageous acceptance of the cruel hand fate had dealt her had moved her far more than she would have believed possible, the more so because it only seemed to emphasise her own feeling of helplessness.

She drew a deep breath, feeling frustration turn to

anger. All those years of medical training to become a doctor, and she hadn't known what to say to the Hammonds. She had let them down, medical science had let them down. Surely in this day and age. . .?

She was scarcely aware of the tapping at the door until it opened and Niall came into the room, his presence the catalyst for so many warring emotions within her that she stared at him with mutinous, tear-filled eyes.

She had forgotten that he was off duty until her vision cleared sufficiently for her to take in the fact that he was wearing a dark suit, the jacket unfastened to reveal a white shirt. For a moment, she found herself wondering who was going to be the lucky recipient of those devastatingly good looks.

She rose to her feet and began returning books to the shelves, her movements oddly uncoordinated. Right now she had enough to think about without letting her imagination run riot where Niall Grant was concerned. What was it about him, that he only had to be near for her natural calm professionalism to fly out of the window?

She frowned with concentrated interest at the titles in front of her, seeing nothing. 'Is there something I can do for you?' she snapped peevishly.

One dark eyebrow rose. 'I've obviously caught you at a bad moment. I can always come back later.'

'No——' she cleared her throat '—it's all right. I'm sorry, I just have a bit of a headache, that's all.' Her heart wasn't feeling too steady either! 'What can I do for you?'

Niall dropped a book on the table and stood with his hands in his pockets. He didn't exactly look like someone who hadn't had any sleep. 'It occurred to me that you might not have seen Madeira before,' he said.

Her interest caught, she smiled hesitantly. 'No, I haven't, but I've been hearing a lot about it, and I've read books, of course.'

His slow smile was doing things to her already overworked pulse-rate. 'Books can't compete with the real thing, though, can they?'

No, they can't, she thought. In books everyone always lived happily ever after. Lovers walked hand in hand towards the sunset. Right now, she thought, with rare cynicism, books had a definite edge on real life.

'I'm sure you're right.' Without her even being aware she was doing it, her fingers rearranged the items on the desk. 'I fully intend being up at dawn to see the ship dock. I have my camera with me so that I can take some photographs.'

'That wasn't quite what I had in mind.' Niall studied her, a frown drawing his dark brows together. 'Lindsey, what's wrong?'

She moistened her lips, wishing there was some way she could avoid his shrewd gaze, but his hands caught at her arms as she tried to turn away. It was as if he had touched a nerve, sending tiny shock waves running through her. 'I don't know what you mean. I've already explained, I have a headache, that's all.'

'You're not a very good liar. Something must have happened.' His gaze narrowed. 'What is it? Has something. . .someone upset you?'

Not nearly as much as his nearness was upsetting her nervous system now, she thought. She stiffened, trying to pull away. It was crazy, she scarcely knew this man, yet he seemed to have the power to throw all her normally perfectly well-adjusted emotions into turmoil.

'It's nothing.' Her shoulders slumped. 'If you really want to know, I just feel I didn't handle a particular situation very well, and it made me wonder. . .' She broke off, raking a hand through her hair with a sigh of frustration. 'If you must know, it made me wonder what sort of doctor I am, that's all.'

'Are you saying you gave an incorrect treatment?'

'No, of course not!'

His mouth twisted. 'Then I think maybe you'll have to explain.'

Lindsey stared at him for a moment, then shrugged. 'The truth is, I've broken one of the first rules of being a doctor. I've allowed myself to become emotionally involved. Dammit, the patient handled things better than I did!'

'Look, ease up a bit,' he prompted. 'Which patient are we talking about?'

'Anne Hammond. She came to see me with her husband.' Lindsey gestured towards the papers on the desk. 'Those are her medical notes and a letter from her GP. The rest are reports of hospital visits going back over eighteen months.'

He reached for the file, flicking through the pages, frowning as he looked up. 'I have to say, the prognosis doesn't look good.'

'The prognosis stinks!' Her eyes blazed. 'That nice lady sat there explaining to me that she hadn't long to live. Her husband clearly adores her.' She broke off, feeling the tears well up in her eyes, willing them not to fall. 'They sat there holding hands, apologising to me because they didn't want to be any trouble.'

Niall was watching her, a frown drawing his dark brows together. 'Why are you blaming yourself? You didn't cause her condition. You didn't diagnose it.'

'Aren't you being just a little simplistic?' she snapped. 'Of course I didn't. I just didn't know what to say. I almost went to pieces. They were nice people.'

Suddenly his hands closed over her arms. 'You're not thinking rationally.'

Lindsey strained backwards, her hands against his chest as she tried to push away from him. Frustratingly his grip merely tightened, sending a tingling awareness surging through her. She resisted it. Some females might like that sort of strong-arm tactic, but she wasn't one of them. 'I'm being perfectly rational,' she bit out. 'The Hammonds are young. They should have their whole lives in front of them, but then you're a man, and men are always rational, always tough. Or maybe you just don't care?'

She knew she had gone too far when his eyes narrowed to glittering blue slits.

'And what makes you such an expert on men?' he demanded. 'Or is it all talk? Maybe we'd better find out.'

For an instant she thought of running, but knew it wasn't even an option as his grip tightened and he drew her, struggling towards him. She braced herself, her face flaming as her body made contact with his, then she was fighting in earnest as the sheer physical awareness of his body tore through her. She struck out at him with her fists until, with a grunt of triumph, he twisted his hand in her hair, jerking her head back, bringing tears of pain and frustration to her eyes. For a moment panic widened them as he lowered his head and his mouth took possession of hers with an aggressive thoroughness, forcing her lips apart as his tongue invaded the soft vulnerability of her mouth.

She gasped at the easy way in which he took advantage of her lack of physical strength to fight him. Then, to her everlasting shame, a new and totally unexpected sensation found its way into her consciousness, so devastating, so unlike anything she had ever experienced before, as her body betrayed her with its instant response.

'Maybe you don't know as much about me as you think,' Niall said huskily, a wealth of controlled feeling in the way he held her from him to look down at her. 'A little knowledge can be a dangerous thing, Lindsey. You should always be sure of your facts.'

Facts! Right now she wasn't even sure what day it was.

He bent his head and kissed her again.

Moaning softly, she swayed towards him, surrendering to an overwhelming need. For an instant she felt him tense, then she was free, his breathing harsh as he drew away. She looked up, startled, a protest beginning to form, then became dizzyingly aware of the open door.

'Ah, Niall, glad I caught you!' Jim Lewis's voice intruded into the tension.

Only then, as the brilliant colour swam into her face, was Lindsey aware of Niall, shielding her from the other man's gaze, gaining her the precious seconds she needed to recover.

She dragged a hand through her hair, only too aware of how she must look. Her mouth felt bruised and swollen, her hair a wild tangle where his fingers had raked through it. All in all, she felt as if she had been ravaged!

'Not called at a bad moment, have I?'

'Not at all.' The sardonic gleam in Niall's eyes wasn't lost on Lindsey. 'I was just clearing up a few points with Dr Blake.' He turned to her. 'I think I've made my position quite clear, wouldn't you say?'

Lindsey straightened her shoulders, purposely avoiding his gaze. 'Perfectly, thank you, Doctor.'

'I'm sure you'll wish to bear it in mind, for future reference.'

She choked. 'I'm sure there's no danger whatsoever of my forgetting. . .' But he was gone, leaving her talking to the air.

She turned to Jim, with an effort managing to keep her voice even. 'I'll see you this evening. I'm looking forward to it—I think.'

His mouth quirked. 'It's really not so bad, as these things go. You get used to them after a while. Personally I've always enjoyed meeting the passengers socially. I've even got to think of a few of the regulars as friends over the years.'

Lindsey assumed a mock frown of disapproval. 'I thought the idea was that we're here to work, not to enjoy ourselves.'

Jim gave a wry chuckle. 'How are you and Niall getting on, by the way?'

'I'll survive.' She gave a light laugh. Maybe not unscathed, the thought intruded. 'I'm still finding my way around, but mostly I'm enjoying it.'

Jim grinned. 'I know you and Niall didn't exactly get off to a good start, but if it's any consolation you caught him at a bad time. He's usually pretty fair.'

'I'll take your word for it.' Lindsey flashed him a look, zipping her document case to a close with unwarranted vehemence. Damn! Since when had Niall Grant become a consideration in her life? 'How long have you been with the ship?' she asked.

If he was aware of her deliberate attempt to change the subject, Jim gave no sign of it. 'I joined about seven years ago, shortly after she was commissioned.'

'You must enjoy the life.'

'It has its ups and downs.' He grinned. 'No, seriously, it suits me. I enjoy the travel, meeting people, seeing different places, but then I don't have any commitments ashore.'

Lindsey felt her heart give an extra thud. 'Yes, I imagine it's not so easy for those who do. I suppose that's why Niall is so much against personal involvements among the crew. He must miss his wife and family.'

Jim shot her an amused look. 'It depends what you mean by involvements. As for Claire, as I remember it, she's a great believer in the theory that absence makes the heart grow fonder.'

A huge, suffocating cloud seemed suddenly to be hovering above Lindsey's head. Niall was married!

Even though she had tried to prepare herself for the possibility, the sense of shock hit her like a physical pain. With an effort she managed to force her lips into a smile. 'They must be the lucky ones. It takes a very special sort of relationship to be able to withstand constant absences.'

Jim gave a loud hoot of laughter. 'I suppose you could say that.'

Lindsey stared at him. 'I don't understand.'

'Claire took off a couple of years ago. Niall arrived home on leave to find she'd packed her bags and left him a note. I gather it was short and not too sweet, running something along the lines of, "I've met some-one·else." The divorce came through about six months ago.'

Lindsey could hear the deafening thud of her own heartbeat as a sensation of relief swept over her. It lasted as long as it took to bring her breathing back under control. Niall might be free as far as the law was concerned, but he had been the injured party, the one left to pick up the pieces when the woman he must have loved walked out. It wasn't very likely that he was going to want to get involved again, was it?

CHAPTER FIVE

'SORRY to call you out so early.' Jill rose to her feet from behind the desk as Lindsey came into the ward.

She shrugged herself into her white coat. 'You did the right thing. What's the problem?'

'Well, we had a member of crew admitted about. . .' Jill consulted the notes '. . .two hours ago. He seems to have a fluctuating temperature. At first we thought it might be a straightforward dose of flu, but now we're not so sure.' She frowned. 'We've been tepid sponging and monitoring since he was admitted, but there doesn't appear to be any improvement—in fact, I'd say he's marginally worse than he was an hour ago, so I thought I'd better get you to take a look at him.' She led the way through the swing door. 'We've put him in the side ward, just as a precaution.'

'You did the right thing,' Lindsey said reassuringly. 'Even if it is flu, with a little damage limitation we might just prevent the rest of the ship going down with it.' She reached for a stethoscope. 'Let's take a look at him. By the way, what's his name?'

'Kewal Patel. He's been with the ship about five years.'

'Right, and he was admitted about two hours ago.'

Jill nodded, standing aside to let Lindsey precede her into the small side ward.

Kewal Patel was about thirty-five. He lay huddled

beneath the blankets, his eyes closed. He was shivering violently.

'Yes, I see what you mean.' Lindsey leaned forward, her fingers gently probing beneath the man's jaw. 'Mr Patel, can you hear me? I'm Dr Blake. I gather you're not feeling too well.'

The man groaned.

'I don't think you're likely to get much more of a response,' said Jill.

Lindsey straightened up. 'What was his temperature?'

'At the last check, a hundred and five.'

'It's possible it could be flu. Has he complained of a headache at all?'

'Apparently. A couple of days ago, and of feeling shivery.'

'Any other pain?' asked Lindsey.

'We haven't been able to get any more information out of him.'

Lindsey drew the covers back, gently but firmly palpating the man's abdomen. She frowned. 'Any vomiting?' Jill shook her head. 'OK, let's have a listen to his chest. It's just possible there could be an infection lurking.'

Seconds later she straightened up, shaking her head. 'Well, that seems clear.'

'So what do we do?' asked Jill.

'First of all, keep him isolated, at least until we know just what we're dealing with here. We're going to need a blood film.'

'I've already seen to that,' said Jill. 'It went down to Jim in the path lab. I stressed that it was urgent.'

'Good for you!' Lindsey glanced at her watch. 'I

know it's early, but I'm going to give Niall a call to arrange a case conference. This could be straight-forward. On the other hand, we can't afford to take any risks, and Niall may have more experience of this type of thing.'

Going through to the office, she put through her call. It was answered almost immediately.

'Niall? I'm sorry to disturb you so early. . .'

'Lindsey, what's wrong?'

'I'm not sure.' She was glad to hear her voice sounding so calm. 'We had a patient admitted a couple of hours ago, presenting with flu-like symptoms, but I'm not happy about him.'

'I'll be right there.'

True to his word, minutes later he walked into the office. His hair was standing slightly on end, as if he had forgotten to comb it, and he wasn't wearing a tie, and it was ridiculous the way her heart lurched just at the sight of him, Lindsey thought.

'You'd better fill me in on the details,' he said.

Putting as much professional coolness into her voice as she could muster, she proceeded to do so, leading him into the side ward, where he could study the patient for himself.

'This is Kewal Patel.' She handed him the notes. 'He's a ship's engineer. It seems he first complained of a headache and feeling shivery a couple of days ago. Someone brought him down to the hospital a couple of hours ago, and since then his condition has deterio-rated. The symptoms are vaguely flu-like, as I said.'

'But you're not convinced?'

'No.'

'Right, let's take a look.'

She watched as he made his own examination before straightening up. 'Well, I'd say your instincts are right. Has anyone else presented with the same symptoms?'

Lindsey shook her head. 'Not so far.' She looked up at him. 'You think it could be some kind of viral infection?'

'It's possible, but I'd lay odds it isn't. I take it you've done an examination?'

'Yes, before I rang you. There's evidence of spleno-megaly, enlargement of the spleen, and of the liver. I've ordered a blood film, stat.'

'Good girl,' he said approvingly. 'Any conclusions?'

She bit her lip, conscious of the colour racing into her face at the unexpected praise. 'Malaria?' she said hesitantly.

He gave a soft laugh. 'Ten out of ten, Dr Blake! Go to the top of the class. The question is,' he sobered, 'what are we going to do about it?'

'You've come across it before?'

He nodded. 'Not often, but yes. It's not so prevalent these days, thank goodness.' He consulted the man's notes. 'I see he spent his last leave at home in Pakistan, visiting his family. Well, that could explain it. Even taking his regular anti-malarial drugs, it can still happen. Anyway, we'll start him on a combination of chloroquine and primaquine. Give supportive nursing care. He'll need daily blood tests, and we'll have to watch for any respiratory or renal involvement. But I'm pretty sure we'll be able to knock it on the head.'

'I'm grateful,' said Lindsey as they walked towards the office.

'You were doing just fine without me.'

Now wasn't that the truth?. she thought, as she watched him striding away.

Lindsey was putting the finishing touches to her notes when someone tapped at the door and a dark-haired girl popped her head round.

'Hello! Can I have a word, or would you rather I came back later?' Advancing into the room, she gave a wry smile. 'Sorry about the gear.' She was wearing a large, baggy cardigan over a luminous pink leotard and tights. 'I've just taken an aerobics class and didn't have time to change.'

Intrigued, Lindsey smiled. 'No, of course not. Now is fine.' She indicated the chair. 'Sit down. As a matter of fact, I've just finished. I was just catching up on some paperwork. Or. . .' she broke off uncertainly '. . .or was this a professional visit?'

The girl laughed. 'No, strictly social. Well, almost. I've been meaning to introduce myself, but you know what it's like.' She mopped her face and throat with the towel she had draped round her shoulders. 'Once we leave port everything takes off. I've been organising classes. . .' She broke off, laughing. 'I'm Kay Jackson, physiotherapist and aerobics tutor — and yes, the two are compatible.' Her smile was infectious. 'I like to think passengers leave one of my classes feeling fit and ready for anything, not as if they've personally helped dig the Channel tunnel! Anyway,' she reached out a hand, 'I know it's a little belated, but welcome aboard.'

'Thank you.' Lindsey shook the proffered hand, smiling.

'Any time you fancy a work-out, feel free — the gym is on deck five. We've got all the equipment, weights, cycles, rowing machines, or if you fancy something a little less strenuous, I take an aerobics class every morning around eleven. Well, when I say less strenuous, I mean you leap in at the level that suits. We cater for all ages, shapes and sizes. Not,' Kay added cheerfully, 'that you look as if you need it.'

Lindsey laughed. 'Not yet, maybe, but a couple of weeks of unbridled gluttony with the sort of food they serve here, and I could be a serious candidate! I may well take you up on the offer.' Sealing an envelope, she dropped it into the basket of outgoing mail. 'So, what was the other thing?'

'Other? Oh yes, I had a gentleman turn up for some physio on his arm. Apparently he was involved in an accident at work a few days ago, went to his local casualty department who couldn't actually detect any break and treated it as a severe sprain.'

'You're not happy about him?'

'Not really.'

Lindsey frowned. 'You think they may have missed something?'

'Well, it's possible. Hairline fractures don't always show up, do they? Anyway, there's certainly no way I'm going to start physio on him the way things are, or at least until you or Dr Grant have given him the OK.'

'He's obviously complaining of pain or discomfort,' Lindsey commented.

'He's not the complaining sort.' Kay gave a slight smile. 'But I'd guess he is. Mind you, he probably just doesn't fancy the idea of spending the rest of his holiday with his arm in plaster.'

'I can't say I blame him. Still, better safe than sorry.'

'My thoughts exactly, which is why I thought I'd have a chat with you.'

Lindsey rose to her feet, nudging a drawer to a close. 'Tell you what, see if you can persuade him to come down for an X-ray. If there is a fracture it's possible it may show up more clearly now, in which case I'm afraid we won't have any choice but to put it in plaster. If not — well, at least he'll be reassured.'

'Will do.' Kay was on her feet, already heading for the door. 'And thanks a lot.'

'My pleasure.' Lindsey followed her out, pausing at the reception desk to hand in her mail and the patients' cards. 'Any more for me?'

Zoe Travers, the medical receptionist, grinned. 'Sorry, can't oblige.'

'Don't tell me I've scared them all away,' Lindsey joked.

'More likely everyone's too busy getting ready for the captain's reception tonight.'

'It's obviously quite an event.'

'One of the highlights of the trip for a lot of the passengers. You'd be surprised, some of them make bookings with the beautician and hairdresser even before they come on board.'

'Oh lor'!' Lindsey ran a hand through her own hair. 'I didn't think.' The French plait she wore was fine for everyday, but she hadn't given a thought to the more social occasions. 'I'd better go and put my head under the shower and make use of some conditioner. I hadn't realised the effect the sea air could have on your hair.'

'Why don't you just ring through to the hairdresser now? Or better still, pop down there?' suggested Kay.

'But I don't have an appointment.'

The other girl smiled. 'I'm sure they'll find time to fit in a member of staff, especially a newcomer. We all know what it's like, having to learn the ropes.'

Lindsey smiled gratefully. 'In that case, I may just do that.'

Contrary to all expectations, ten minutes later she was seated at the washbasin, and forty minutes after that she emerged from the salon feeling refreshed and certainly different.

Her thick honey-blonde hair, freed now of its plait, brushed against her neck in silky waves. Her nails had been manicured and lightly touched with colour, and her cheeks, slightly flushed, seemed somehow to add emphasis to the startling green of her eyes. Her steps were surprisingly lighter as she made her way back to medical reception.

Zoe greeted her arrival with a slightly harassed look. 'Oh, Doctor, I've just had a call from Cabin 226—a Mrs Jeffreys. Her husband isn't feeling too well.'

Lindsey paused in the act of unclipping her bleeper. 'Any specific symptoms?'

'Mm, let's see. Mainly high temperature and sore throat, slight nausea.'

'I'd better go straight up there.' Lindsey glanced at her watch. 'Bother! I'm due to do a ward round. . .'

'That's all right.' Niall spoke from the doorway. 'We're not exactly rushed off our feet. I'll cover for you.' He was wearing jeans and a black sweatshirt, revealing tautly muscled shoulders. His damp hair was slicked back as if he'd recently been for a swim or taken a shower.

Lindsey found herself battling against an almost

overwhelming and totally illogical desire to run her fingers through its neatness.

She swallowed hard. 'No, really, there's no need. I may be a few minutes late, but I can make it.' She gave a slight grimace. 'Barring anything unforeseen.'

'Easier if I do it. At least that way it won't delay anyone going off duty.' He paused, looking her over with swift assessment. 'You've done something to your hair — I like it. You should wear it loose more often.'

She resisted the urge to lift a hand to it. 'It's all right for a special occasion. I don't think it would be practical on a day-to-day basis.' It was frustrating to discover that his nearness could make her feel so vulnerable. 'I'd better go and see Mr Jeffreys.'

'Lindsey, wait!' Niall's hand caught at her arm and she found herself being drawn towards him, the pressure of his fingers light but insistent. It was disconcerting to hear the slow thud of her own heartbeat sounding heavily in her ears.

She drew herself up sharply. 'Will it wait? I'm going to be late,' she said edgily, and saw his dark eyebrows raised quizzically.

'It won't take a minute. It's about tonight — I should have mentioned it earlier but forgot. I'd like you to join us, after the reception, at the senior medical staff table in the restaurant, for dinner tonight.'

'Dinner?' Lindsey queried.

'The reception. You haven't forgotten?'

'No, of course not.' She gave a slight laugh. As if she could!

Blue eyes narrowed. 'So you'll join us? You know we always invite a number of passengers to join us?'

She bit at her lower lip, stifling a feeling of rising

panic. This was a one-way track, leading nowhere. With an effort she managed to look at him and smile.

'Thanks for the offer,' she said briskly. 'It sounds nice and I appreciate it, but if it's all the same to you, there are a few things I need to catch up on. You know what it's like. I'm still finding my way. . .'

'Obviously I didn't make myself clear,' said Niall with sudden dry impatience. 'It wasn't an invitation. The first night on board, everything is deliberately kept informal, to give passengers time to settle in and find their bearings. But after that there are certain formalities where members of crew are concerned.' He frowned. 'Senior officers, and that includes members of the medical team, are expected to dine with invited guests. Socialising with passengers goes with the job, Doctor. It isn't an option, it's a privilege.'

Lindsey felt the colour flooding her cheeks. How could she have been so foolish as to imagine he had issued the invitation on a personal level? 'I see.' Her voice wavered. 'In that case, yes, of course I shall be happy to join you.'

'Good. In that case I'll see you later.' He strode away without giving her a chance to speak, leaving her with the distinct impression that she had just been steamrollered.

'Now there's a sight for sore eyes!'

She blinked and looked up, smiling, as Jim wandered into the room with a handful of X-rays. 'Flatterer! I bet you say that to all the ladies!'

'One has one's reputation to keep up. In this case it just happens to be true.' Grinning, he dropped the films on to her desk. 'I thought you'd want these. The appropriate reports are attached.'

She flicked through them. 'Anything serious?'

'No. A couple of straightforward minor fractures, one sprain. Why do people on holiday suddenly start taking up the kind of violent exercise they wouldn't even contemplate normally?' sighed Jim.

Lindsey gave a slight smile. 'Maybe they're all thwarted deck quoits champions? Or maybe they've never had the time before. Who knows?'

'Ah, Jim.' Zoe popped her head round the door. 'Sorry to intrude, but there's a call for you. It's the pharmacy—a query about a prescription. Would you like me to transfer it through to here?'

'No,' he waved a sheaf of papers in the air, 'I'd better go and see to it in person.' He headed for the door, pausing to look at Lindsey. 'Don't forget, I'll pick you up. Just before eight? Then we can have a drink in the bar first.'

'That's fine, I'll look forward to it,' she managed evenly.

If you had to walk into the lion's den, better have someone on your side. Though why she should need any kind of defence against Niall Grant was a question to which there seemed no logical answer.

Within a matter of hours it seemed the weather had changed. The breeze had a milder edge to it, the sea was calm, unlike her own thoughts. Lindsey found her hands gripping the deck rail as she gazed out at the golden track made by the fading sun on the water.

Having seen Mr Jeffreys and diagnosed an acute and fairly painful dose of tonsillitis, she had intended going straight back to her cabin, instead of which, without even being aware of it, she had walked in the opposite direction. The last thing she needed right now was to be alone with her thoughts.

Shivering, she realised the light was beginning to fade, and almost reluctantly she turned to make her way back inside.

After a leisurely afternoon tea, most of the passengers were in their cabins, either relaxing or preparing for the evening's entertainment. Lindsey fought off the realisation that she should be doing the same, a tiny spark of rebellion taking her, instead of to her cabin, to the gallery of luxurious and well-stocked shops and boutiques, carrying everything from souvenirs and jewellery, famous brands of perfume and toiletries to designer shoes and clothes.

She hadn't actually intended to go in, but the window display caught her eye and, without thinking, she wandered in, to look, certainly not to buy, until she realised with a pang of guilt, as she gazed at the racks of colourful fashions, that everything in her wardrobe must be hopelessly out of date.

The truth was, she thought with a pang, that since Paul had ceased to be part of her life she hadn't felt the desire or the need for any kind of social life, apart from the occasional visit to a pub with colleagues. As a result of which, she had to acknowledge ruefully, everything in her wardrobe, while it might be of good quality, was strictly practical.

Then she saw the dress, and before she knew it she was trying it on. The price tag made her wince. It wasn't as if she really *needed* it, as if there was anyone she wanted to impress. . .

Back in her cabin, the dress on a hanger, she indulged in a leisurely soak in her favourite perfumed bath oil in an effort to make herself relax. Twenty minutes later she stood in front of the mirror wearing the fragile lace undies which were also the result of her impulse-buying. She was going to have to stop this, she told herself firmly.

Her make-up she had purposely applied slightly more heavily than she would have done during the day, silver-grey shadow adding emphasis to her eyes, a touch of blusher for her cheeks, lipstick. Small gold hoop earrings caught the light as she turned her head.

The effect, when finally she slipped into the black dress, was both dramatic and startling. A little too startling, maybe? Doubts came rushing in as she stared at her reflection, wondering what on earth had possessed her to buy it. It was unlike anything she had ever owned before.

The bodice clung to her breasts as if it had been moulded to her, a thin diamanté halter giving an illusion of safety. As she moved, the fabric clung to her hips, and the skirt was slashed at the front from knee-level down, so that as she walked it gave a glimpse of her dark-stockinged legs.

Staring at her reflection, she realised she must have lost weight. A few months ago she would have needed to buy a larger size, but it looked good, she had to admit. Even if it didn't, it was a little late to do anything about it.

She was applying touches of her favourite perfume to her pulse points when, right on cue, someone tapped at the door. That would be Jim.

Slipping her feet into slender-heeled sandals, Lindsey reached for her evening purse and went to open the door.

'Come in. I just have to get my jacket and find my bleep. Help yourself to a drink. I won't be. . .'

She broke off, feeling a rush of heat and cold all at the same time as Niall studied her with penetrating intensity. She felt the glittering sweep of his blue eyes flame over the creamy translucence of her bare shoulders to the curve of her breasts.

'You!' She swallowed convulsively on the sudden tightness in her throat. 'I. . . I was expecting Jim.'

'Sorry to disappoint you,' he said evenly. 'Something came up, an urgent lab report.' Lindsey wondered if she had imagined the note of satisfaction in his voice. 'He asked me to make his apologies.'

CHAPTER SIX

LINDSEY passed her tongue over her dry lips, intensely aware of him, the musky tang of his expensive aftershave. 'I see. Well, in that case, you'd better come in.'

Heat flooded through her body as he took the jacket she was holding from her hands. If she had thought him attractive before, he was devastatingly so now in the black evening suit. The whiteness of his shirt seemed to emphasise his tan, but it was something in the glittering gaze, raking her slowly from head to toe, that made her hesitate.

'Is something wrong?' She stared down at her dress, blushing as she remembered how little she was wearing beneath it. 'You did say it was a formal reception.'

'You look fine,' he told her huskily. He draped the jacket round her shoulders, his hands briefly making contact with her flesh. She couldn't prevent her tiny indrawn breath. An involuntary shiver ran through her, and as if he was aware of it, something flared briefly in his eyes before he released her. 'I think we'll forget the drink.'

His gaze narrowed as he held the door open. 'There's no need to be nervous—it's just a reception.' He smiled, and the effect was devastating. 'That's not to say you won't get waylaid by the odd passenger who wants to discuss his medical history!'

'I'd say that's par for the course.' She avoided his gaze, glad that he had mistaken the real reason behind that shiver. He was still too close. She could feel the warm strength of his body against hers as he ushered her out of the cabin, one hand against her back as the lift doors opened. Niall Grant was the most disturbingly sexually arousing man she had ever met, and his nearness was affecting her in a way she hadn't dreamed possible.

The lounge was crowded as they entered, pausing in the doorway to join the queue of people waiting to be introduced to the captain.

John Carlisle was a good-looking man of about fifty, his smile genuinely welcoming as he reached out to clasp Lindsey's hand.

'Dr Blake—Lindsey—I've been looking forward to meeting you. Niall's been telling me something about you. We must get together some time for a chat. I'm afraid we're a little crowded in here,' he confided with a wry smile. 'Circulate, enjoy yourselves.'

Niall's hand propelled her forward. 'There, that wasn't too bad, was it?' He raised a mocking eyebrow and she felt the colour flare into her cheeks.

'Been telling tales out of school, Dr Grant?' She couldn't resist aiming the jibe.

'One thing I can promise you, Dr Blake,' he said softly, 'I never kiss and tell.'

Lindsey choked. 'Why, you. . .'

'Tut, tut!' His mouth quirked. 'Language, Dr Blake! Remember we're in company.'

She bit her lip on a response, conscious that he had, once again, had the last word.

There were certainly more people than she had expected as they edged their way into the crowded lounge. A band was playing and the room was filled with chattering groups, waiters gliding between them with trays of fruit juice and champagne-filled glasses, others with canapés.

Lindsey stood in the doorway, conscious of a sudden tension in her limbs, a feeling of blind panic that made her want to draw back.

Just when she had thought she was beginning to get her feelings about Paul into some sort of perspective, the memories came flooding back to haunt her.

Rationally she knew it was over. There would be no more hideous scenes, no more humiliating accusations. But, irrationally, for those few fleeting seconds the fear still rose, threatening to choke her.

Without even being aware of it she had half turned, her eyes widening with panic, only to feel the gentle but firm pressure of Niall's hand beneath her elbow.

'Are you all right?' Blue eyes looked down into hers.

She swallowed hard on the tightness of her throat, the momentary fear vanishing, to be replaced by a far more tangible awareness of the man standing beside her. It was ridiculous to feel safe with someone who, in every other sense, seemed to represent a threat, even though she couldn't have said precisely what that threat was. But the feel of his hand against her back was like a protective barrier, drawing her to him, shutting everyone else out.

'I should have warned you about the crush.' His brows furrowed briefly. 'I think I'd better lead the way.'

She followed, taking several deep breaths, releasing them shakily. Almost immediately Niall was waylaid, and involuntarily she found herself searching for his dark head in the crowd.

'Lindsey!' A glass of fruit juice was thrust into her

hand. 'We've been keeping an eye open for you.' It was Jill, her face flushed, her eyes unusually bright. 'Come and meet a few people. This is Tony, by the way.'

Lindsey found herself shaking hands with a tall, fair-haired young man and wondered if she had imagined the tension which seemed to be sparking between the two.

'I've been looking forward to meeting you,' she smiled.

'Same here.'

Before she knew it she was being drawn away, guarding the glass in her hand, then Jim was at her side. 'Sorry about that, *cariad*, but Niall needed an urgent report at the last minute. Have you had any food?'

'Not yet.' Her brow furrowed on the realisation that it was Niall who had been responsible for the last-minute change of plans. Funny—he hadn't said anything about that. She had to raise her voice above the noise, gazing in admiration at the buffet. 'It looks almost too good to eat! That isn't *real* caviar?'

'The very best. Try it.'

She did, and pulled a face. 'Personally I think it's overrated,' Jill laughed as they moved along the table, Lindsey helping herself to food she didn't really want. She caught sight of Niall, watched as he threw back his head and laughed. At that moment he looked in her direction, and the blood raced in her veins.

Don't be ridiculous! she chided herself. He's a good-looking man, and the smile just happens to be part of the job. She averted her eyes, draining the glass of fruit juice in one gulp.

'Shall we get out of this crush?'

The note of quiet desperation in her friend's voice drew Lindsey's gaze to Jill's flushed face, causing her own smile to fade.

'Are you all right?' she asked anxiously.

Jill grinned and took a deep breath. 'I just need some fresh air, that's all.' Abandoning an untouched plate of food, she headed for the nearest door.

Lindsey followed, sighing her own relief as the noise faded behind them. She turned to the other girl and was surprised to see a glint of tears. 'Look, it's pretty obvious you're upset,' she said gently. 'Would it help to talk?'

The other girl gave a shaky laugh as she twirled the liquid in her glass. 'It's ridiculous — I've only just realised how much I'm going to miss all this.'

'Miss it?' Lindsey stared at her. 'But why. . .?'

'Tony and I have decided to get married.'

'Oh, but that's marvellous!' Lindsey was genuinely delighted. 'When?'

'Pretty soon. In about three weeks' time, if you want to be really precise.'

'Well, you certainly don't believe in wasting time, do you? But,' Lindsey frowned, 'doesn't that mean. . . you'll miss the next trip?'

Jill gave a slight smile. 'More than just the next trip. I've decided not to renew my contract. I shall be leaving when we dock.'

'Oh, no!' Lindsey stifled a genuine feeling of sorrow. 'I'm delighted for you, of course. I mean. . .'

Jill laughed. 'I know what you mean.'

'But do you have to leave?' Lindsey broke off, stifling a tiny feeling of resentment. 'You're a damn good nurse. You'll be missed. I know Niall's views on relationships between members of crew, but surely. . .'

'I don't know about that,' smiled Jill. 'And thanks for the recommendation, but seriously, I'm twenty-seven and Tony's thirty-three, and we both want a family. Now seems as good a time as any.' She shrugged. 'I'm not saying it's going to be easy, giving all this up, I mean. On the other hand — ' a grin broke out ' — I quite fancy hearing the patter of tiny feet. My sister had a baby about three months ago, and I met it for the first time when I went home.' She pulled a face. 'I suddenly realised what it is to feel broody.' She broke off as Jim came towards them.

'I wondered where the pair of you were hiding. You don't get out of it that easily.' Grinning, he whisked the empty glass out of Lindsey's hand and swept her, laughing, into his arms. 'I've come to claim my dance.' He executed an intricate jumble of steps.

'I'm not sure I'm up to this,' she protested.

'I'll teach you, *cariad*. Just follow my lead and we'll have them standing in the aisles.'

'Roaring with laughter, I should imagine.'

His attractive face assumed a pained expression. 'I'll have you know I was the scourge of our local Pontypool dance hall every Saturday night.'

'I'm impressed.'

'And so you should be. I have medals, girl, medals.'

'So has my grandad,' said Lindsey, 'and he can't dance either.'

There was something nice and safe about an old-fashioned waltz, she decided, settling into the comfortable circle of Jim's arms as they drifted back to the dance floor. Nothing too demanding, either physically or emotionally.

The music changed to something more up-beat and, as if by mutual consent, they both moved from the floor, weaving their way through the crowd in search of a space.

Unconsciously she found herself searching for Niall. She saw him, deeply engrossed in conversation with the captain and a group of passengers.

She found herself watching, fascinated, as he smiled down at the woman beside him. Of indeterminate age, she could, Lindsey realised, be anything between thirty and fifty. Diminutive, dark-haired, she had the kind of flawless, honeyed skin that any woman would envy, and the sight of Niall's hand, proprietorially against her back, filled Lindsey with an emotion she absolutely refused to acknowledge as jealousy.

With an effort she wrenched her gaze away, forcing her attention to the person who was speaking to her.

'Hello! I've found you at last. I was beginning to think you'd given it a miss.'

It was several seconds before Lindsey recognised the dark-haired girl grinning at her. 'Kay!' she exclaimed.

'Don't say it. You didn't recognise me without the leotard. It happens all the time.'

Lindsey laughed. 'I have to admit, you do look different.'

'Got to keep up the image, haven't we? Besides, how many opportunities to dress up are there these days?'

'The passengers certainly seem to love it.'

'Can you blame them? For most of them, this is the trip of a lifetime. Oh, you get the few stalwarts who come year after year, but for the majority it's their one and only chance to be pampered, to see places they might otherwise never see.'

Kay broke off as a large, blue-rinsed American lady and her cigar-smoking husband joined them.

'Isn't this a wonderful party? And the captain is such a charming man. Why, he actually remembered our names from a year ago! Isn't that just amazing?'

'It certainly is,' Lindsey smiled, forbearing to mention that, as guests filed into the reception lounge to be formally greeted by the captain and his deputy, each couple would have handed their formal invitation card to a senior officer and had their names discreetly murmured into the captain's ear as the introductions were made.

'Of course, we've sailed with the company for several years now, haven't we, Dexter?'

'We certainly have, my dear.'

'In fact, we're staying on at the end of this trip to do the world cruise.'

'How nice!' Lindsey accepted another glass of fruit juice from a passing waiter.

'Mr and Mrs Rossington.'

Lindsey saw a photographer's flashbulb explode in front of her. She blinked, momentarily blinded, then experienced a sense of shock as she realised that her early warning system, that nervous tingle that ran down her spine, had betrayed her as her vision cleared and she realised Niall was standing beside her.

She didn't even need to turn her head to know it was him. For several seconds, as their gazes met and held, she was disturbingly aware of the strong, sun-bronzed column of his throat, the startlingly blue gaze which studied her with an intensity so vibrantly sexual that it almost took her breath away before he turned his attention to the American couple.

'I gather you're going to be joining us for the world cruise?'

Mrs Rossington's cheeks were suddenly very flushed. 'Why, I was just saying. . .'

'It's always a pleasure to see our regulars. After a time we come to think of them as old friends.'

It must be so easy to fall into the habit of saying the right thing, what was expected. Yet, watching him, Lindsey realised that Niall was genuinely pleased.

She was aware of his hand coming to rest against her bare back, the warmth of his fingers stirring her senses in a way she knew to be totally illogical.

His gaze was inscrutable as he smiled at the American couple. 'And now, if you'll excuse us, duty calls, I'm afraid. Unlike yourselves, Dr Blake has only recently joined us, and there are a few people she should meet.' Intercepting a fresh glass of champagne from a passing waiter, he pressed it into Mrs Rossington's hand. 'I look forward to seeing you again soon, though I hope on a social rather than a professional basis.'

It was so skilfully managed that almost before Lindsey knew what was happening the pressure of his hand was drawing her away.

'I think we should dance,' he said.

Lindsey's breathing felt constricted as they moved into the crowd. Why did this man have such an effect on her? It was like nothing she had ever experienced before. And why did the band have to choose that precise moment to play a waltz so that, rather than dancing apart in the modern way, he was drawing her closer, moulding her to the lean, taut length of him?

She could feel the heat of him, the thin fabric of her dress no barrier at all.

She stiffened defensively. 'That wasn't necessary. I didn't need rescuing.'

His dark brows rose fractionally. 'I didn't imagine you did.'

Confusion brought the colour faintly to her cheeks and she swallowed hard, her mouth strangely dry as she was held within the intimate circle of his embrace. His blue eyes were unfathomable depths, making her feel uneasy. Niall Grant was an enigma, and she decided she didn't like enigmas. Far safer when you knew what someone was thinking.

'Relax,' he said softly. 'At least try to make it look as if you're enjoying yourself.'

She was trying, but his proximity was making that impossible. 'I didn't realise this was some sort of public exhibition,' she retorted.

'But it is precisely that.'

'Oh.' Perversely she felt disappointed.

'The theory is that if we set the lead the passengers will overcome their inhibitions and join in,' Niall added.

'Isn't there also something about ship's officers escorting unaccompanied *guests*?'

'I don't actually see any, do you?'

Involuntarily Lindsey glanced over his shoulder and felt his jacket brush softly against her cheek. It smelled of expensive cologne, and her skin tingled as he turned his head, his sensuous mouth drifting warmly, dangerously close to her cheek.

She drew a long, shaky breath. He was certainly right about one thing, she thought. As passengers overcame an initial shyness the floor had begun to fill with dancing couples, the captain among them. But it was his partner who drew and held Lindsey's gaze.

She frowned as an elusive memory flickered and was lost again. 'The woman dancing with Captain Carlisle — I saw you talking to her earlier. There's something about her. . .' Lindsey shook her head and gave a slight laugh. 'It's ridiculous, I know, but I feel as if I should know her, as if I've seen her before somewhere.'

Niall turned to follow the direction of her gaze, a smile touching his mouth as he did so. 'You probably have, only larger than life. That's Adele Duncan.'

'Duncan. . .' Lindsey shook her head. 'Duncan.' Realisation dawned. 'Adele Duncan, the film star?'

His mouth twisted. 'The one and only.'

'Of course. No wonder she looked so familiar!' Lindsey was intrigued. 'I hadn't realised she was so tiny. She's even more beautiful in the flesh than on screen.'

'I'll tell her you said so.'

She was vaguely aware of being guided expertly away from the crowded floor, and it wasn't until they stepped out into the cooler night air that she realised how much of a relief it was to leave the noise behind.

The ship had slowed its speed as passengers gradually began to drift away from the reception to enjoy their evening meal in one of the several top class restaurants.

Lindsey leaned against the rail watching the lights of a passing ship as it plied in the opposite direction. 'Where exactly are we?'

'Exactly?' One dark brow rose quizzically. 'There's a lot of sea out there.'

'More or less will do.' She turned her head, laughing, and felt the sound die in her throat before her gaze skittered away. He was too intensely masculine, too overwhelmingly vital for her not to be aware of him.

Amusement threaded his voice. 'Somewhere past Portugal, and over in that direction must be the north-west coast of Africa. Madeira is about five hundred and fifty kilometres from the Moroccan coast.'

'Africa! That explains why the air is so much warmer.' In the semi-darkness she studied his profile, letting her gaze wander over the hard-boned features, absorbing the line of his jaw, wondering what was going on inside his head. He must think she was babbling like a schoolgirl, but there was nothing even remotely schoolgirlish about her growing awareness of this man.

In desperation she looked away. 'You seem to know her very well — Adele Duncan,' she responded to his questioning gaze.

He straightened up and put his hand under her arm, sending an illogical tremor running through her as they began to walk slowly towards the bow of the ship.

'Adele is one of our regulars, usually on the Transatlantic run. She hates flying.' A brief spasm flickered across his features. 'She always says the cross-ing gives her an opportunity to relax and study her scripts.'

'Nice work if you can get it!' Lindsey's smile flicked up at him. 'I thought she was married, but there doesn't appear to be a Mr Duncan. You'd better watch out; maybe she's looking for husband number four on this trip.'

Instantly, as she sensed the tautening of his muscles, she wished the words unsaid. 'I . . . I'm sorry, I shouldn't have said that, especially as. . .' She broke off, appalled by the realisation that she was getting in deeper still.

'Especially as?' Niall prompted softly.

Lindsey was glad of the semi-darkness that hid the flush in her cheeks. 'Look, I'm sorry. I heard about your divorce.' She swallowed hard. 'It was tactless of me. I didn't mean. . .'

'It's not a problem,' Niall advised her hardly. 'Being a ship's doctor is pretty much like living in a village or any small community. It was hardly a secret.'

Lindsey frowned up at him, moistening her dry lips. 'But surely. . .your wife wasn't. . . I mean, I assumed. . .'

'Claire was the ship's entertainments officer, and she and Adele got to know each other quite well. I suppose they had a lot in common.'

Lindsey stared out at the water. 'It must have been a terrible shock, when she left, I mean.'

He frowned. 'Maybe in this job you get used to the absences. You have to, to survive.'

She turned slowly to give him a long, searching look and decided he must have become expert at keeping his emotions on a tight rein.

'Maybe I should have realised it wasn't the same for Claire. She was a sociable creature; she liked people.' For a fleeting second a hint of cynicism darkened his eyes. 'She obviously decided there was more to life than a ship's doctor had to offer.'

'I'm sorry,' said Lindsey quietly.

'Don't be.' He turned his back to the rail. 'It could have been worse. At least there weren't any children to be hurt by what happened.'

But what about *him*? What about *his* feelings?

Lindsey felt a tiny bubble of anger welling up inside her. 'You say it as if in some way it excuses her,' she remarked.

'Maybe. If I'd seen what was happening, hadn't been quite so involved in my work, I could have done something about it before it was too late.' He sighed. 'I should have realised Claire was unhappy.' He dragged a hand through his hair. 'It can't have been easy for her. We didn't always do the same trips. Sometimes she came home just as I was due to leave, or vice versa. She once joked that we were like ships that passed in the night.'

'But surely she must have known what the job entailed?' she snapped, her anger in no way lessened by the knowledge that it was illogical. 'A doctor, and more especially a surgeon, *has* to be involved.'

'The difference was that, for Claire, the novelty wore off. She wanted to settle down, make a permanent home. It was reasonable enough, but I'd just signed a new contract with the company. In any case, it wouldn't have been so easy for me to start again at something else. Being a doctor is what I do. I suppose I could have settled eventually to general practice or applied to any of the hospitals. But there are plenty of eager young registrars falling over themselves to fill the places.' He shrugged. 'So she met someone who could seemingly give her all the things I wasn't able to.'

Lindsey felt her anger stirring. 'She met him on board ship?'

'He was a hairdresser. I suppose he worked quite closely with the entertainment crew, preparing for shows.'

GET 4 BOOKS
A CUDDLY TEDDY
AND A MYSTERY GIFT

Return this card, and we'll send you 4 LOVE ON CALL romances, absolutely FREE! We'll even pay the postage and packing for you!

We're making you this offer to introduce to you the benefits of Mills & Boon Reader Service: FREE home delivery of brand-new LOVE ON CALL romances, at least a month before they're available in the shops, FREE gifts and a monthly Newsletter packed with offers and information.

Accepting these FREE books places you under no obligation to buy, you may cancel at any time, even after receiving just your free shipment.

Yes, please send me 4 free Love on Call romances, a cuddly teddy and a mystery gift as explained above. Please also reserve a Reader Service subscription for me. If I decide to subscribe, I shall receive 4 superb new titles every month for just £7.20 postage and packing free. If I decide not to subscribe I shall write to you within 10 days. The free books and gifts will be mine to keep in any case. I understand that I am under no obligation whatsoever. I may cancel or suspend my subscription at any time simply by writing to you.

Ms/Mrs/Miss/Mr _____ MVD

Address _____

_____

_____ Postcode_____

Signature_____
I am over 18 years of age.

Get 4 books
a cuddly teddy and
mystery gift FREE!

SEE BACK OF CARD FOR DETAILS

Mills & Boon Reader Service,
FREEPOST
P.O. Box 236
Croydon
CR9 9EL

Offer expires 31st October 1994. One per household. The right is reserved to refuse an application and change the terms of this offer. Offer applies to U.K. and Eire only. Offer not available for current subscribers to Love on Call romances. Readers overseas please send for details. You may be mailed with offers from other reputable companies as a result of this application. If you would prefer not to receive such offers, please tick this box.

No
stamp
needed

Illogically, Lindsey wanted to shake him. 'Do you have any idea where she is now? What she's doing?'

To her surprise he gave a deep-throated chuckle. She felt her heart give an erratic thud as his eyes held hers, heard his soft intake of breath as he turned slowly to face her. 'The last I heard she'd transferred her affections to some aspiring West End producer.'

The pressure of his hand drew her closer. She felt a flood of heat as he stared down at her, felt the deepening intensity of his gaze on her in the few seconds before his mouth descended slowly to take possession of her lips.

An involuntary tremor passed through her. As if he was instantly aware of it Niall raised his head. 'You're cold.'

'No.' Her voice was husky. Cold was the last thing she felt right now. Confused, maybe, but certainly not cold. 'Don't you think we might be missed?'

His warm breath fanned her cheek as he began another teasing foray across her eyelids, her ear, the hollow of her throat. His lips merely brushed against hers, yet it was enough to make her feel as if her entire body was on fire. She could hear the discordant thudding of her own pulse, feel the heat of his body permeating through his suit to her legs, making her all too disturbingly aware of his own arousal.

Confused, she lifted her face to his, a new kind of awareness bringing the colour to her cheeks. His grip firmed on her shoulders, and she was shaken by the feeling of warm strength that seemed to pour into her as he lowered his head to kiss her again.

The sensation was exquisite. Lindsey's head went back. She could hear the muted drumming of her own heartbeat as his mouth claimed hers, cutting off the protest that rose fleetingly to her lips. The kiss was a fierce, stormy possession, making her head swim and bringing with it the realisation that it would take no effort at all to become seriously attracted to this man!

For a second shock held her immobile. It was all happening too fast. The fact that he was kissing her, holding her in his arms, didn't mean her feelings were reciprocated. He had been the injured party when his marriage broke up and, in spite of everything, it was all too clear that he still retained strong feelings for the woman he had married.

Better end it now, a warning voice rang deep inside her brain. You're here to do a job, get on with it as unemotionally as possible. Unfortunately that was easier said than done.

In desperation she drew away, just as the bleep she carried in her purse broke discordantly into the silence.

'I'm wanted on the ward,' she said breathlessly. 'We'd better get back.'

Niall's dark brows drew together. 'Maybe you're right. I'll come with you. I wanted to pick up some reports anyway.'

His voice was rough-edged as he reached to open the door, his hand brushing against her shoulder. Brief as it was, the contact was sufficient to trigger a whole wealth of signals she was working desperately hard to suppress.

Lindsey sighed heavily, wishing she had never met Niall Grant, and knew that even that wasn't true.

CHAPTER SEVEN

THE moment Lindsey opened her eyes next morning she knew that something was different.

She lay for several seconds trying to think what it was, then realisation suddenly dawned. The ship wasn't moving. There was no steady thrum of engines. Some time in the early hours they had reached Madeira.

With an almost childlike whoop of delight she bounded out of bed, quickly stifling the sound as she caught sight of her alarm clock. *Six o'clock!*

Grabbing a robe and a towel, she was heading for the shower when someone tapped quietly at the cabin door. Hurrying to open it, she was greeted by the sight of Kay Jackson, already brightly clad in a pink and white shell suit, breathing hard as she jogged on the spot.

'Hi!' She kept her voice to just above a whisper. 'We've docked. I thought you might like an early morning trot round the crew deck to get your first view of the island.'

'Give me five minutes.' Lindsey grinned. 'This is ridiculous—I'm so excited, you'd think I was five years old!'

'Believe me, I've done the trip half a dozen times, and the novelty of arriving at a new port never wears off.' Kay grinned. 'I don't know why we're whispering! Most of the passengers were either up on deck to watch the ship arrive or they'll be frantically getting organised for an early breakfast so that they can get ashore.'

'How about a quick cup of tea while I shower?' said Lindsey.

Ten minutes later, dressed in aqua-coloured jogging pants and a white T-shirt, her hair vigorously tamed into a ponytail and with trainers on her feet, Lindsey stepped out on to the crew deck into bright May sunshine and a temperature of seventy degrees. The sea was a brilliant blue millpond.

'Isn't this fabulous?' Lindsey gave up all pretence at jogging as she grasped the rail to get her first glimpse of Madeira.

Already, on the dock below, taxis were lining up, waiting for passengers who might want to tour the island independently, rather than join the organised excursions by coach.

Kay was right; even at this early hour the ship was a hive of activity. Some of the passengers must have been up just after dawn to watch the huge liner ease its way gently alongside the dock, and those who weren't were beginning gradually to emerge on the upper decks, or to enjoy breakfast by one of the pools.

Lindsey lifted her face to the sun. 'Mm, you can actually smell the air! It's like. . .perfume!'

'That will be the flowers. Things we think of as exotic grow wild here, like the mimosa. You'll see it everywhere, and the orchids are a sight to behold. Madeira is a volcanic island and the temperature stays at roughly seventy degrees all year round,' Kay told her, 'so it's just perfect. Like a huge hothouse.'

'Don't!' Lindsey pulled a wry face. 'You make me wish I were going ashore.'

The other girl looked at her with an expression of dismay. 'Can't you?'

'Someone has to be on call.' Lindsey tried to stifle a note of wistfulness. 'I'm it.' She eased herself away from the rail. 'It can't be helped—it's just one of those things. The system is worked out to be fair to everyone. Anyway, who knows, I may get the odd half-hour just to pop down the gangway and explore those fascinating little shops down there.' She glanced at her watch. 'We've just about got time for a quick swim before breakfast.'

'Not for me, I'm afraid.' Kay shook her head, stifling a yawn. 'The stalwarts will be queueing up for their jog round the deck.'

'But you've already done it once.'

'Ah, but that was for *me*.' Kay's white teeth flashed in a smile. 'Look, I'll catch up with you later. I'm hoping to get ashore after lunch for a while, but we may still get that swim. We don't sail till this evening, so things will probably be fairly quiet.'

'I shall look forward to it.' Watching the other girl jog into the distance, Lindsey hesitated fractionally before deciding that she might as well go for a swim anyway. If nothing else, it would help to clear her head and, just now, she relished the thought of being alone.

After the previous evening, too many conflicting emotions seemed to be crowding in on her, and she wasn't sure she knew how to deal with them, or indeed, she thought, stepping out of her jogging pants and T-shirt to reveal the figure-hugging jade-green swimsuit beneath, whether there was anything to deal with, other than her own imagination.

The pool on the crew deck was deserted, and Lindsey wasted no time before diving in head first from the side. She was a strong swimmer, and spent five minutes ploughing her way effortlessly along its length before surfacing to sleek her hair back and knead the water from her eyes. It was almost a relief to discover that even in the short time she had been on board ship she was already beginning to acquire a golden tan.

Flipping lazily on to her back, she floated with her eyes closed for a moment, frowning as the sound of a door closing echoed around the pool. So much for peace and quiet! With a tiny frown of resentment she rolled over again, took a breath and dived soundlessly to swim below the surface for one final lap.

She had made it halfway before deciding to come up for air, turning her face upwards as she broke the surface only to collide in a tangle of arms and legs, with a strong, masculine body.

Coughing and spluttering, she went under, treading water, and suddenly found herself supported by a pair of equally strong arms as she fought for the surface.

Gasping, momentarily blinded by the water in her eyes, she became conscious of Niall, treading water beside her, of his dark hair, plastered against his head, of his bronzed, naked chest against which her own head was resting as he let the water take her weight, drawing her towards him.

'All right, don't panic. I've got you.'

Panic? Who was panicking? Lindsey gasped as her legs made contact with his thighs, a shockwave running through her as his hands moved to encircle her waist.

Blushing furiously, she trod water as she ran her hands awkwardly through her wet hair. 'You! I didn't think anyone else would be using the pool this early.'

'Mostly they don't. I usually have it to myself.' His

body drifted towards hers. 'This is my favourite time of day, before the rush starts, when everything is quiet.'

'Sorry to intrude.' Her voice sounded oddly husky. Through her half-closed eyelids she could see the tiny droplets of water glistening on his skin. His hair was slicked back and she could see the powerful shoulder muscles ripple as he took her weight.

'You're not intruding.' His gaze travelled to rest on her face. 'It's not every day I find a mermaid in the bath.' The surface of the water barely rippled as he drew her effortlessly towards him.

There was a buzzing in her ears. Too much water, Lindsey told herself, as a dizzying surge of awareness started the warning bells ringing in her brain again. This was not finding a solution to her problem. He *was* her problem, and an irrational sense of panic was setting in. Unless she was prepared to take second place in his life.

Her hands rested against his chest, making a fragile barrier between them. She should put a stop to this now. What had happened to her willpower? She closed her eyes, as if by doing so she could shut him out of her mind.

Temptation wasn't so easily resisted. His arms encircling her waist, Niall seemed to raise her effortlessly. She was briefly conscious of the wet swimsuit emphasising every curve of her body, then she was lowered again, her breathing uneven as his brooding gaze levelled with hers.

Put your foot down, she told herself weakly as he pulled her gently towards him. But she was already out of her depth, in more ways than one!

'I should be going,' she muttered.

'Yes,' he murmured softly, and his mouth found hers. Worse and worse! It was like being washed up by the tide and left stranded. Half a love surely had to be better than none at all?

For what seemed an eternity their bodies moulded together. Lindsey could feel the steady build-up of desire until she knew she had to break away. Where were all the resolutions she had spent most of the night making?

Her hands against his chest, she pushed backwards, breathing hard.

'Lindsey!' he groaned, reaching out for her.

It would be so easy to give in, simply to take what was on offer. But what about when it was over? His nearness was creating havoc, robbing her of the power to think. She had to get away.

Panic gave her the strength to break free, and she struck out for the side of the pool. Swallowing convulsively, she rubbed vigorously at her face and hair with a large bath towel until her skin burned. She reached for one of the freshly laundered robes which were supplied each day for users of the pool.

Watching Niall haul himself out of the water, she felt suddenly absurdly shy as, in one fluid movement, he bent to retrieve his own towel, draping it casually around his neck.

If anything, the sight of a half-naked Niall out of the water was even more devastating than Niall in it, Lindsey decided, tearing her gaze with difficulty from the stunning perfection of his body in the briefest of black swimming trunks.

The incredible thing was that she guessed he had no idea of the impact he made, or simply didn't care.

'You're a surprisingly strong swimmer for someone of your slight build.'

She jumped as he held out her robe, helping her slip into it. How long had he been standing there watching her? she wondered, feeling the colour surge into her cheeks.

'I enjoy it. I'm not sure it's quite the same thing. As a matter of fact, I came up on deck to get my first glimpse of the island. From what I can see of it, it must be quite spectacular.'

'It is,' he mused evenly, and she had the uneasy feeling that he knew she was deliberately trying to change the subject. 'Have you made arrangements to go ashore?'

'I'm on duty,' she reminded him, smiling wryly. 'Still, next time, maybe.' If there was a next time. She reached briskly for her tote bag. 'At least I remembered to bring a camera with me. With a bit of luck I'll be able to get some good shots from the top deck before we sail.'

Niall frowned. 'You're not on duty twenty-four hours.'

'No, of course not,' she gave a light laugh.

'In that case, there's no reason at all why you shouldn't go ashore.'

Lindsey stared at him. 'But someone has to be on call, surely? Not all the passengers go ashore.'

'The majority will,' he said evenly. 'The few who decide to stay on board can still attend normal surgeries if they feel it to be necessary, and the likelihood of a real emergency developing in the meantime is pretty remote. In the event that one does arise we still have a senior medical crew on board, and I always carry a radio pager. So there's no reason at all why you shouldn't have a few hours off. As a matter of fact, I shall be going ashore myself after lunch.' His tone was suddenly cool and brisk. 'I shall have finished the crew surgery by midday. You should have done the ward round by then. We'll go together.'

'But. . .' Lindsey swallowed hard on the sudden restriction in her throat. 'I can't let you. . .'

'Nonsense! I'll be waiting.' He seemed suddenly to have lost interest. 'Gangway number three, one o'clock. Don't be late.'

As if she would dare! Lindsey stifled a sigh as she watched his retreating figure. Why did she get the distinct impression that she had just been steamrollered?

Reception was noticeably quiet when Lindsey made her way there later. Only one of the seats provided in the waiting area was occupied, and the girl behind the desk greeted Lindsey's arrival with a smile.

'Not much chance of being rushed off your feet this morning.'

'So I noticed as I came through.' Smiling, Lindsey peered at the list. 'What have we got?'

'Two so far. Mr Lane outside, and this one. . .' Zoe pointed at the second name '. . .was just a request for something for an allergic rash. I explained that I couldn't actually prescribe and that he'd need to see you. I don't think he was too happy about it.'

'No,' Lindsey smiled. 'Well, I can't say I blame him.' She frowned. 'So where exactly is he?'

Zoe laughed, nodding in the direction of the consulting-room. 'Waiting for you.'

'Oh, right,' Lindsey grinned. 'In that case I'll see him now, then he'll be able to go ashore.'

The second patient was equally swiftly dealt with. 'I'm going to give you a course of antibiotics, Mr Lane—you've got quite a nasty ear infection there. Your throat is slightly inflamed too.' Lindsey dropped a spatula into the wastepaper bin and returned to her desk. 'It must have been bothering you for a few days.'

'It has been a bit painful, but I thought it would probably go away if I ignored it, so I didn't bother seeing my own doctor before we sailed.' Mr Lane smiled his relief as he took the prescription. 'I'll know next time.'

Smiling, Lindsey escorted him to the door. 'It's always best not to take chances with ear conditions. Usually the problem is quite minor, but anything particularly painful or persistent should always be checked. Anyway, enjoy your day ashore. Oh, and I'd stay out of the swimming pool for a few days if I were you, unless you can keep your head above water. Best to give the tablets a chance to do their stuff,' she advised.

'Will do.' Waving the prescription, he went happily on his way.

Lindsey was clearing her desk when someone tapped at the door. Certain that Zoe had said there were no other patients, she frowned, then was instantly on her feet as Anne Hammond appeared, standing hesitantly in the doorway.

'Mrs Hammond. Is something wrong? You're not. . .'

'Oh, no, no.' The woman's fragile face broke into a smile. 'I didn't mean to worry you. . .'

Lindsey felt her stomach muscles relax. 'That's all

right. Come in, sit down.' She motioned her towards the chair, surreptitiously studying the young woman's pale features, noting the deepening of the shadows beneath her eyes. 'How are you feeling?'

'A little tired, but that's to be expected, and I don't regret a thing,' came the firm response. 'This trip is everything I dreamed it would be and more. Everyone is so kind. The food is. . .' She raised her hands and laughed. 'What can I say? It's out of this world. Our cabin is marvellous, and on top of that, I'm going to see places I've only dreamed about until now.'

'You're not overdoing things?'

'Probably, but I want to make the most of every minute. You don't really realise how precious time is until it starts running out.' Anne Hammond smiled. 'Steve and I are going ashore.'

'Has someone arranged for a wheelchair?'

'It's all taken care of. The reason I'm here is that I'm running a little low on tablets. We're always so careful, but. . .well, I suppose we were so busy getting ready for the cruise. . .' Anne Hammond broke off. 'I don't like having to leave everything to Steve. He has enough to worry about.'

'It's no problem.' Lindsey was already reaching for her pad. 'I'll write you up for some now. The pharmacist will make up the prescription and get them delivered to your cabin. They'll be waiting for you when you get back on board.'

'I appreciate it, really.' Anne Hammond was on her feet. She tucked a strand of hair behind her ear. The pale yellow skirt and sleeveless top she wore seemed, somehow, to emphasise her fragility. 'You've been very kind. Everyone has.'

Lindsey swallowed hard. 'That's what we're here for. But look, if you feel. . .'

'It's all right,' the girl smiled. 'One of the nurses is coming ashore with us—she offered. I didn't want anyone to go to that sort of trouble, but. . .well, I know Steve's worried, and I want him to enjoy this trip.' She turned, her hand on the door handle. 'I'd better go, before he sends out a search party or something.'

'Call me if you need me when you get back.'

'I will.'

The door closed behind her and Lindsey sat for several minutes, trying to bring her feelings and emotions firmly back under control, finally having to hurry to carry out her ward round.

'Hello.' Jill greeted her arrival, completing the notes she was writing before clipping her pen into the pocket of her dress. 'Are you going ashore?'

'I hadn't actually planned to,' Lindsey shot her a wry look, 'but yes. I'm told Madeira is an experience not to be missed, so I've been coerced.'

'I should jolly well think so!'

'How about you? Going to buy a few souvenirs to take back home?'

'You must be joking! Any more and I could set up shop!' Two spots of colour appeared in Jill's cheeks as she reached for the report book. 'No, I may just pop out to one of the local cafés by the dock, but I shan't tour the island, not this time. Anyway,' she rose briskly from her seat behind the desk, 'I'm on duty pretty well all day, so it's not really feasible.'

'No, I suppose not.' Lindsey smiled. 'How is Tony?'

'He's fine,' said Jill. 'Anyway, this isn't getting the round done. The sooner it's finished, the sooner you can get away. I don't think there's anything too much to worry about, so you can enjoy your afternoon with an easy conscience. Mr Warren is still with you. You remember he was admitted yesterday afternoon with slight respiratory problems?'

'That's right.' Lindsey studied the card. 'He has a touch of bronchitis and he's what. . .sixty-two?' She frowned. 'How is he responding to the antibiotics? No side-effects or anything?'

'None so far; in fact he seems quite a lot brighter this morning.' Jill's smile was genuine this time. 'In fact he's champing at the bit. He wants to get ashore, and who can blame him? No one gets stuck in a hospital bed from choice, least of all on holiday.'

Lindsey chuckled. 'Yes, well, that's natural and a good sign.' She unwound the stethoscope from her pocket. 'I'll check him over now. Keeping him in overnight was just a precautionary measure because of his age and past history, but I don't see why he shouldn't go, provided he keeps up the antibiotics. I'll see him first.'

'Right. Apart from Mr Warren, there's just Mrs O'Donnell.'

'That's the diabetic lady whose urine test gave some cause for concern.'

'That's right,' Jill agreed.

'You've done another test?'

Jill nodded. 'I've also had a chat with her, and it seems she didn't think it necessary to let us know about her condition when she came on board. I think she imagined if she didn't think about it it might go away. The result you can see for yourself.'

'She obviously hasn't been too careful about what

she's been eating.' Lindsey sighed. 'It's difficult, faced with the marvellous food on offer twenty-four hours a day. I suppose she knows the chef can cater for diabetics and there's absolutely no reason why she should have to feel she's being denied any of the luxuries?'

'Precisely what I told her. I've also had a word with the catering officer and given Mrs O'Donnell a diet sheet. She seems much happier.'

'So, provided the next urine test is OK, I see no reason why she can't be discharged as well,' said Lindsey.

'She'll be pleased to hear it.' Jill finished writing her notes. 'I think we'd better go, don't you, before we have a mutiny on our hands?'

An hour later, after a light salad lunch, Lindsey made her way back to her cabin. There would just be time for a quick shower if she hurried.

Feeling refreshed, she changed into pastel pink shorts and a baggy white sweater with matching pink motif. Her legs had begun to acquire a nice, even tan, and she slipped her feet into a pair of sandals before brushing her still damp hair into a ponytail. Tossing her sunglasses and some local currency into a tote bag, she found herself having to make a dash up to the top deck, arriving to find Niall leaning against the rail.

He was dressed casually in jeans and a white, baggy shirt, unbuttoned at the neck to reveal the strong, tanned column of his throat. He turned at her approach, every fluid movement of his lean body an enticing reminder of his earlier powerful near-nakedness in the pool. Lindsey swallowed hard. Her defences were already activated and registering red alert, and he hadn't said a word yet!

He turned and seemed to take stock of her, the unwittingly defensive stance of her slim figure, and she found the experience highly disconcerting.

'I'm sorry I kept you waiting,' she managed breathlessly. 'I got held up at the last minute.'

'Don't worry about it, I only just got here myself.' He looked her over with swift assessment, and, ridiculously, she found herself wishing she had worn something less revealing than the shorts, but it was too late to do anything about it now. 'Ready?'

She flushed as a glint of humour flared briefly in his eyes. Studiously avoiding his gaze, she jammed her sunglasses firmly on to her nose.

'I can't wait! Where are we going?'

'I thought you might like a guided tour of the island. It will have to be the shortened version, I'm afraid, but you'll be surprised how much we can cover in a few hours.' Niall held out a hand to steady her as she stepped off the gangway on to the dockside. 'I hope you're feeling energetic?'

Lindsey clenched her teeth. 'Just lead the way!'

Which turned out to be towards a taxi, one of the few remaining on the dockside now that most of the passengers had gone ashore.

She watched with rapt fascination as Niall approached the driver, who greeted him with a flashing grin of recognition.

'Hey, Doctor! *Bom dia*.' He tossed away a cigarette as the two men clasped hands. 'I wait for you, like always. You want go somewhere good to eat? A bar?' His glance went appreciatively to Lindsey, who felt herself blush. 'Somewhere quiet, maybe?'

She heard Niall say something softly in the man's

own language, watched the other man's smile widen as he nodded.

'This is Dr Blake—Lindsey Blake. Lindsey, this is Jesus, pronounced *Hayzoos*,' Niall smilingly enunciated for her benefit. 'Jesus and I have got to know each other quite well over the years. Like the rest of the drivers, he knows when each of the cruise ships is due in and he usually waits for me to go ashore. I've explained that you'd like to see something of his island.'

'Oh, yes, very much, *por favor*.' Lindsey smiled shyly, as they moved towards a battered black car which was parked close by.

'This is Dr Blake's first visit to the island. I'd like her to be able to see as much as possible, without rushing.'

'Ah, *sím*. You leave to me—I show.'

The car door was opened and Lindsey found herself being ushered into the back seat, and with his usual masculine grace Niall climbed in beside her. The proximity of his thigh next to her own sent an unexpected tremor running through her.

'Comfortable?' Niall reached over to take her tote bag, placing it on the floor. As he did so his hand accidentally brushed against her bare leg, and suddenly she was aware of how little difference there was between the shorts she was wearing now and the swimsuit she had worn earlier.

'I'm fine, thanks.' She turned her head quickly to stare out of the window.

It was like a journey into paradise, Lindsey thought, as the taxi left the dockside to begin a steady climb into the hills. It sounded childish, she knew, but she was unable to prevent the tiny gasps of pleasure as her eyes were assailed at each new turn by ever more glorious sights.

The main street was lined by trees, heavy with swathes of blue blossoms. 'Oh, look—they're beautiful!' she exclaimed. 'What are they?'

'Jacaranda,' smiled Niall.

'I've heard of them, but this is the first time I've seen them like this. I'd no idea they'd be so lovely.'

Gazing from the window of the taxi, she watched the small groups of tourists, many of them from the ship, strolling in and out of shops eagerly purchasing souvenirs.

Jesus half turned to point out something. '*Mercado dos lavradores*,' he said.

'He says it's the local farmers' market,' Niall translated. 'It's where the local people come each day to sell their produce, flowers, vegetables, fruit. You'll find a few fish stalls too. The fishermen's quarter is down by the quayside, along with some of the best seafood restaurants. In fact, you'll find very little meat on the island. The locals eat mainly fish and vegetables.'

Jesus waved in the direction of one of the stalls where fish were arranged on beds of ice. '*Lulas, atum, mariscos.*'

Niall grinned. 'Squid, tunnyfish and shellfish.'

'A nice healthy diet.' Lindsey watched in fascination as the taxi laboriously made its way along the rising curve of the road taking them into the hills.

Everywhere, on rock faces and in crevices, exotic flowers bloomed in profusion like weeds—mimosa, antirrhinum, hydrangeas. At one point, as the ancient taxi manoeuvred a particularly narrow twisting stretch of road, she found herself gazing into a steep-sided gorge. Involuntarily she reached out, blushing as she realised her fingers were clamped firmly on to Niall's thigh.

Swallowing hard, she released her grip. 'I hadn't realised Madeira actually had mountains and cliffs.'

'Don't worry about it. Jesus knows these roads like the back of his hand. The island is actually the summit of a huge, extinct volcano. A bit like the tip of an iceberg.' He leaned forward, saying something to Jesus, and seconds later the car drew to a halt in a lay-by.

'We're stopping!' Lindsey said, surprised.

'There's something I think you'll want to see.'

Niall's hand supporting her, she climbed out, following him to stand by a stone wall, then gasped at the sight of the vast blue sunlit curve of the bay now far below them.

'It's beautiful!' she breathed. 'I hadn't realised we were so high up. Oh, look, I can see the ship.' She darted a look at Niall's profile, only to find him studying her in a way she found oddly disturbing. 'I'm sorry, you should have stopped me. You must have seen this dozens of times.'

He stared down at her and her pulse-rate accelerated dangerously. 'I never tire of it,' he murmured, close to her ear. 'There's always something new to see.'

The heat seemed to be having a heady effect on her, Lindsey thought faintly. His arm brushed against her, setting her heart thudding.

'I think we'd better move on.' His voice was uneven. 'We've a lot more ground to cover.'

Jesus was leaning against his taxi. He flicked away another cigarette as they made their way towards him to continue the drive still higher into the hills.

They stopped at an orchid farm, spending an hour just wandering through vast greenhouses, filled with blooms of every conceivable colour and variety, some headily perfumed, others with no scent at all.

'I wouldn't have believed there were so many varieties.' Lindsey's eyes danced with pleasure as she emerged finally, clutching a bag of the large tubers which were sold to tourists. 'I couldn't resist.'

Niall's dark brows rose mockingly. 'Got a large garden, have you?'

'So I'll buy some windowboxes,' she declared stoutly.

'Here, you'd better let me.'

'No, it's fine. I can manage.'

But he had taken the package from her, and somehow, in the process, drawn her towards him. Her eyes widened with confusion. She felt him tense, then he was tipping up her face and kissing her very slowly and with a thoroughness that left her head reeling.

'If you knew how much I've been wanting to do this.' His voice was uneven as he raised his head, running a hand through her hair to lift its silken weight from her neck.

Her hand rested against his chest, the strong, lean body so tantalisingly close. She tried to move away, disturbed by the realisation that her feelings towards him had undergone a subtle change even though she couldn't quite define it.

'I'm not sure this is a good idea.' Her voice sounded strangely husky. 'What if a party of tourists comes along?'

'I don't think it's likely.' He cleared his throat as if it was suddenly troubling him. 'I'm not even sure I care.'

Lindsey sensed him tensing, then found herself

watching in rapt fascination as his mouth descended again. 'Please, don't,' she protested weakly.

He cupped her face in his hands, moaning softly as he drew her resisting body towards him. 'Don't fight me, Lindsey. Surely you must know the effect you have on me?'

How could she not know? The pressure of his kiss deepened in what seemed like a powerful and shocking invasion of her senses. Her hands tensed against the solid wall of his chest. She heard the sharp intake of his breath and desire flared out of control so that, despite herself, she responded.

They clung together, her body offering no resistance as his mouth became more ruthless, more demanding, creating a desire in her so strong that she moaned softly. She wanted him. It was like nothing she had experienced before.

Her arms reached up, her hands entwining in the thick darkness of his hair, drawing him closer until their bodies merged in a force so powerful in its intensity that it was almost frightening, and a new, even more disturbing sensation forced its way into her bemused senses.

His fingers linked with hers, drawing them to his lips where he turned them to kiss her open palm.

She gasped at the exquisite sensation it aroused and tried to snatch her hand from his grasp. But instead of releasing it he began to kiss each finger in turn until he came to the pale circle on the third finger of her left hand.

His blue eyes looked into hers. 'There was someone?'

'I was engaged,' she said steadily. 'His name was Paul.'

A brief hardness flared in his eyes. 'Tell me about it.'

'There's nothing to tell.'

'Why did you leave him?'

Lindsey smiled quickly. 'What makes you think I did?'

'Because no man in his right senses would let you go.'

She looked away. 'We were both medical students. He qualified a year ahead of me.' She found herself talking quite calmly. 'We shared the same interests, had the same circle of friends.'

'What went wrong?' asked Niall.

She stiffened as his persistent probing began to stir more deeply, memories she had imagined were safely buried. 'Possibly we grew up. I don't know.' She paused as words momentarily failed her. 'Things were fine as long as we were just friends. It was when we became engaged that things seemed to change. He became. . . too proprietorial. I didn't realise, at first, that my friends were gradually being pushed away, until it began to happen with my family too.' She looked at him, sensed an inner anger as he muttered something beneath his breath. Her fingers clenched.

'Did you love him?' he asked, relinquishing them.

'I thought so, at the time.' A slight shiver shook her slim frame, though it had nothing to do with feeling cold. 'Obviously I was mistaken.'

Gentle fingers lifted her chin and began to trace the outline of her mouth. 'It wasn't your mistake, Lindsey. Sometimes we just have to learn to let go.'

She was beginning to lose control beneath the feather-light touch of his fingers against her cheek and eyes. She stood very still, her eyes closed, afraid he might see what was happening to her. She had imagined she loved Paul. It was only now that she began to realise that her feelings bore no relation to what she was experiencing now, with this man.

She tensed with the need to resist the powerful feelings he was evoking. This was crazy. What had happened to all her resolutions not to get involved?

Whimpering softly, she tried to break away, but his grasp merely tightened on her shoulders, firing warning signals in her brain.

'I think we should be getting back,' she muttered hoarsely.

'Lindsey, wait!' His hands raked through her hair, tracing the curve of her breasts, her waist.

'Please, don't make this any more difficult than it is,' she pleaded faintly. Physical attraction was one thing, love was quite another. It needed a two-sided commitment and, willingly or not, Niall was already committed, to another woman.

But—the thought hit her like a wave—it was already too late. She was in love with Niall Grant.

'I want to make love to you.' The touch of his fingers set every nerve-ending on fire. 'I need you.' He tried to draw her back into the circle of his arms.

Need, want. Lindsey felt her throat tighten. But there was a world of difference between wanting and loving.

She pulled away, her soft mouth trembling, her eyes dilated and vibrantly green in her flushed face. 'But don't you see?' she protested. 'None of this is real.'

'Not real!' He gave a harsh laugh. 'I never felt more alive, more aware, and I know you want me.'

'But that's just it, don't you see, we're falling into a trap. Take a look around you. It's a ready-made paradise.' Her voice sounded drugged and heavy from the feelings she was so desperately trying to bring under control.

'You're not making sense, you know that,' Niall growled thickly.

Lindsey shook her head, pushing weakly against him. 'That's the point. Neither of us is thinking rationally. It would be too easy to let ourselves get carried away, do something we might regret later.'

She was aware of his taut face, frowning down at her. 'I. . . I'm sorry.' She pressed a hand against her mouth, blushing as she realised the buttons of her T-shirt were unfastened. She drew them together quickly.

'Don't be,' he rasped. 'I'm the one who should be sorry.' A nerve pulsed in his jaw then, abruptly, he released her. 'You're right, we should be getting back,' he said.

They drove back to the ship in virtual silence, sitting apart like total strangers, she thought, turning her head to stare unseeingly out of the window.

This was ridiculous. She swallowed on the sudden constriction in her throat. Common sense told her it was better this way—ended now before anyone got hurt. Some things were best avoided, and Niall Grant definitely came into that category.

But, ridiculous or not, it didn't explain why she should feel so cheated.

CHAPTER EIGHT

LYING awake that night, Lindsey sighed, tossing restlessly as her mind refused to switch off the events of the day. Glancing at the clock, she sighed and lay back against the pillows, an arm flung across her eyes. She should be getting some sleep, she told herself irritably, not lying here trying to erase the memory of a very disturbing kiss from her mind.

You did the wise thing, calling a halt when you did, she told herself sharply for the umpteenth time. But somehow, wisdom and logic seemed to have very little to do with anything, especially at two o'clock in the morning!

Seconds later, it seemed, someone was shining a very bright, warm light against her closed lids. With a sigh of irritation she floated reluctantly back to consciousness.

Morning! Brilliant sunlight. Another bright new day, full of challenges. Groaning, Lindsey reached for her robe, padded to the bathroom and stuck her head under the cold shower.

Overnight, as passengers slept soundly in their cabins after a long day ashore, or the more hardy danced and gave in to the temptations of the midnight buffet, the *Ocean Empress* had weighed anchor and begun to move south again, until, shortly after dawn, the silence of the engines pronounced her arrival in Tenerife off the west coast of Africa.

121

By eight o'clock, as Lindsey made her way to the hospital, the sun was already hot and getting hotter, and the excitement of the previous day was being repeated as passengers hurried to go ashore.

The purser's office was busy as she made her way through the ship's main reception area, and a queue of passengers needing to make last-minute purchases of local currency had formed. Everyone was cheerful and dressed for the sun.

Jill was shaking down a thermometer as Lindsey walked on to the ward. Her face wore a slight look of concern, and she made a note of the reading before looking to smile a brief acknowledgement of Lindsey's arrival.

'I thought you might want to take a look at young Timothy here. His mum brought him about half an hour ago with a pretty nasty cut on the head.'

Lindsey looked down at the child lying on the examination couch and felt the breath catch in her throat. His eyes were closed, his face was pale. He couldn't have been more than five years old, she realised with a sense of shock.

Blood matted the blond hair, and Lindsey took a deep breath as she leaned closer to peer at the wound. It was certainly a nasty gash.

'Mm, it doesn't look very nice, does it?' Her hand shook slightly as she reached for a swab, and the child began to whimper as she gently began trying to clear the affected area in order to get a better look.

It was ridiculous, but somehow she had never overcome a resistance to working with children. Their vulnerability was like a gaping hole in the cloak of professionalism she had always otherwise been able to

build around her. Even in medical school it had inhib-
ited her to the point where she had even had serious
doubts about whether she would be able to continue
her studies, simply because, unlike many of her senior
colleagues, she had never quite managed to acquire the
kind of detachment that was so necessary sometimes to
become a doctor.

'Any idea how it happened?' she asked.

'Apparently he was having a race round the deck
with one of his friends and managed to slip and fall
down the stairs.'

Lindsey reached for a fresh swab. The child let out a
howl of fright, pushing at her hand, and she blinked
hard, biting at her lip, starting suddenly as she became
aware of the figure suddenly standing beside her.

Niall's coat brushed against her arm as he peered
over her shoulder. 'I heard there was a bit of an
emergency. I was on my way down anyway.' He leaned
forward, and the faint smell of expensive aftershave
assailed her nostrils, adding to a feeling of dizziness.
'Any vomiting or loss of consciousness?'

'No,' said Jill.

It was amazing really, Lindsey thought, watching,
fascinated, as the child's tears became a hesitant smile.
She drew in a sharp breath.

'Are you all right?' Niall asked casually.

She felt the colour stir in her cheeks. 'Yes, fine. It
must have been too much heat or. . .something.'

'It happens. I'll bet you'll have a pretty nasty headache, won't you, young man?' He smiled down at the
child, drawing a tearful smile in response. Niall reached
for an ophthalmoscope. 'Shall we take a look at your
eyes, just like this.' He shone the light into his own

eyes first. 'I promise you, it won't hurt a bit. Well, you're lucky,' he announced, seconds later. 'That's a pretty hefty bump you have there, but it won't need stitches.' He looked at Jill. 'Butterfly sutures should do the trick, though obviously we'll need to check on it again. A dressing should help to keep it clean.'

One small hand emerged from beneath the sheet to probe the area where a large bruise was already forming. 'It hurts, here.'

'Yes, I bet it does,' Niall said sympathetically. 'But nice Dr Blake here is going to make it feel better, and I think, to be on the safe side, you'd better stay with us for a while, just so that we can make sure the headache doesn't get any worse. I'll be along to see you again later. In the meantime, why don't you try to get some sleep?'

Timothy nodded, winced, then closed his eyes as Niall rose to his feet, moving away from the bed. Lindsey followed him to the desk.

'Poor little chap, he's not very happy, is he? Where's his mum?'

Lindsey swallowed hard in an attempt to clear her throat of its sudden restriction. 'Look, I'm grateful for what you just did. I. . .' She was appalled to feel her eyes fill with tears, blinking them away furiously. 'I don't know what. . .'

He leaned across, cupping his hand under her chin, and said softly, 'Don't be afraid of your emotions, Lindsey. There's nothing wrong with crying. I've done it myself.'

He didn't say for whom, but she could guess.

He lowered his head and kissed her fleetingly on the

mouth. Her lips parted, hesitantly, beneath his, then she stiffened and pulled away.

He sighed, straightened up and glanced at his watch. 'I must go. Call me if you need me.'

It needed an effort to turn to Jill, to force her mind back to what she should be doing.

'I suggested his mum go and have some breakfast with the rest of the family while we got young Timothy settled. Ah,' Jill looked up, smiling, 'here she is now! Mrs Saunders, this is Dr Blake.'

Mary Saunders looked anxious and sounded breathless. 'How is Timmy? He's going to be all right isn't he? I got back as quickly as I could. The others were all getting ready to go ashore when it happened.'

'There's nothing to worry about,' Lindsey was quick to offer the smiling reassurance. 'He's going to have a pretty bad headache for a while and the cut is pretty deep, so it's bound to be sore. But we've given him a thorough going over and I'm sure it's nothing more serious than a mild concussion.

'Oh, no!' wailed the mother.

'You really don't need to worry. The young are amazingly resilient. But what I would like to do is to keep him here, just for the next few hours. That way we can keep an eye on him and make sure he doesn't get up to anything too strenuous. Not that I think he'll feel like doing much of anything for a few hours, anyway.' Lindsey smiled. 'I've written him up for some medication to ease the headache.'

'I'd like to stay with him, if that's all right?'

'Yes, of course it is, if that's what you want. But my guess is that he'll sleep most of the morning and probably wake up feeling much better. Obviously you're most welcome to stay, but it seems a shame to disrupt your day.' Lindsey smiled at the woman. 'Look, Sister Reynolds is our specialist when it comes to looking after children.' She glanced at Jill. 'Is Helen on the ward now?'

'I think she's actually doing a medicine round. Would you like me to fetch her?'

'Would you?' Lindsey nodded. 'I think it might help to put Mrs Saunders' mind at rest if she knows Timothy's in good hands.' She turned to the woman again. 'Look, why don't you go ashore as planned? Spend the morning doing some sightseeing, pop back to the ship for lunch and come in to see Timothy then? He'll have had a chance to sleep. His headache should be lots better. Who knows, he may even feel well enough to get up and enjoy some lunch with you.'

Mrs Saunders looked anxiously from one to the other. 'You really think so? But I feel so guilty. . .'

'There's really no need,' Jill intervened, smiling. 'It's not as if you can do anything—and believe me, we've enough staff who'll be more than happy to keep him occupied if he should wake up, but just now all he wants to do is sleep. I doubt if he'll even notice you're not here.'

'Well. . .' Mrs Saunders smiled wistfully. 'I really was looking forward to going ashore. . .'

'You've come a long way to do just that.' Lindsey looked at her watch. 'Look, if you go now you can do a lot of sightseeing between now and lunchtime. Timothy may even feel well enough to spend the afternoon by the pool, provided he doesn't try to do anything too energetic, like diving, for instance.'

'Don't you worry, I'll make jolly sure he doesn't!'

Jill clipped a pen into her pocket. 'I tell you what—he's dozing right now. Why don't you take a peep at him, just to put your mind at rest? I'll come with you and introduce you to Helen, Sister Reynolds, at the same time.'

Lindsey watched as the two made their way up the ward. She was in the office writing up her notes when Jill came back alone, her mission obviously accomplished.

'Everything OK?' she asked.

'Fine.' Jill grinned. 'Young Timothy is sleeping like a top and Mum seems quite happy. Mind you, I suspect she'll only stay ashore for a couple of hours, but that's better than nothing at all.'

'Talking of which,' Lindsey closed the medication book, 'what time are you going ashore?'

'I hadn't thought about it,' said Jill.

'You must be looking forward to getting your feet on solid ground and doing some sightseeing for a change.'

Jill smiled, reaching up to stack a box of sterile supplies into a cabinet. 'Some of the others missed shore time in Tenerife on their last trip, so it seems only fair they should go this time. Anyway,' she focused her attention on the list she was checking, 'I'm not worried. I thought I might catch up on a few chores instead. You know how it is—there's never enough time.'

Lindsey grinned. 'You're going to throw away a chance to get away from the ship for a while? The sea is blue, the sun's shining. It must be eighty degrees out there.'

'I've seen it all before,' came the cheerful response.

'Besides, I quite fancy the idea of just lazing around with my feet up.'

'You're looking a bit peaky. A change of scene would do you good. Even a large ship like this can become claustrophobic if you don't get away once in a while,' said Lindsey.

'Well, I'm glad to hear someone else agrees. I've been trying to talk some sense into her.'

At the sound of the voice coming from behind her, Jill jerked forward, scattering the boxes she had been stacking. 'Tony—damn! Now look what you made me do!' Furiously she began gathering them up, two spots of colour highlighting her cheeks as his hands came down over hers.

'Butterfingers! Remind me not to need stitching when you're on duty.' He flashed a smile in Lindsey's direction. He looked attractive, she thought, in the dark trousers and the white short-sleeved shirt.

Smiling, she turned away, concentrating her gaze on the notes she was writing in an attempt to distance herself.

'I thought you wanted to do some shopping,' Tony murmured.

'Yes, I do.'

'Didn't you mention something. . .lacy and delicate. . .'

Jill aimed a blow at his arm. 'I was talking about tablecloths.'

'So was I,' he tutted softly. 'Why, Sister Stewart, what did you think I meant?'

'I know precisely what you meant, but I told you, I'm still on duty.'

'Look, you two,' Lindsey broke in, smiling, 'why

don't you go and do your shopping? Some of us have work to do.' Rising to her feet, she gathered up a sheaf of files. 'I have to be here anyway, and it doesn't need two of us to cover, so why not take a couple of hours or so?'

'See?' Tony insisted. 'Someone's on my side.'

Jill gave an exasperated sigh. 'Why do I get the feeling I'm outnumbered here?' She glanced, frowning, in Lindsey's direction. 'Are you sure you don't mind? Only there's some absolutely fabulous local lace. . .'

'I told you, I'm more than happy to cover. Anyway, I really do need to catch up on some paperwork, so you'd be doing me a favour.' Coward! a tiny inner voice insisted. If she were really honest, she didn't want to run the risk of seeing Niall again for a while, not socially at any rate. 'Go and enjoy yourselves,' she said. 'Maybe then I can get on with some work. Talking of which,' she glanced at her watch just as the phone rang, 'I shouldn't be here.'

Automatically Jill reached over to answer it. 'Hospital, Sister Stewart. . . Oh, yes. No, no, I'm afraid Dr Grant isn't here at the moment, but I have Dr Blake with me. Yes. . .yes. Look, try not to worry. Someone will be with you immediately.'

'Problem?' asked Lindsey as Jill replaced the receiver.

'Could be. That was Adele Duncan's secretary. She sounded a bit fraught. Apparently Miss Duncan is having some kind of attack, and she asked for Niall.'

Lindsey was instantly alert. 'Did she say what kind of attack?'

Jill pulled a face. 'It was all a bit garbled. Something

about breathlessness, chest pain.' She met Lindsey's gaze. 'Could be a heart attack.'

'Do you know where Niall is?'

'As far as I know, he's still working his way through the list of cabin calls, then he was due to do a routine hygiene inspection. He certainly hasn't reported back yet.' Jill reached for the rota. 'He's due at a crew meeting in about an hour, so he shouldn't be too long.'

Lindsey glanced again at her watch. 'We can't risk waiting.' She was already reaching decisively for her briefcase. 'I'll go along there, just to be on the safe side. Tell you what, you hunt through the file, see if we have a case history on Miss Duncan. It might give us a head start, just in case we have to admit her.'

'Will do.' Jill was already on her feet as Lindsey left the office.

Making her way up the stairs to One Deck, Lindsey tapped at the door of the Empress Suite. From inside she could hear raised voices and a shrill cry, as if someone were in pain.

A sense of alarm prompted her to knock again, more loudly, and this time the door was thrust open by an elegant though plainly dressed young woman who winced at the sound of breaking glass, coming from somewhere behind her.

'You requested the attendance of a doctor. I'm Dr Blake — Lindsey Blake.'

A brief flicker of uncertainty crossed the carefully made-up features. 'Oh, well, you'd better come in, though I'm not sure. . .'

'Who is it, Morton?' called a voice.

'It's the doctor, Miss Duncan.'

'And about time too!' The voice sounded surprisingly

strong for someone supposedly in the throes of a heart attack, thought Lindsey, stepping into the suite and only with a real effort stifling an exclamation of amazement. The Empress Suite was one of the most sumptuous accommodations on board, more like a penthouse apartment than a suite.

'Can you give me any details?' Lindsey slipped back into an air of professionalism.

'She's having a bad day,' came the wry explanation.

Lindsey motioned towards the bloodstained tissue wrapped round the secretary's thumb. 'You're hurt!'

'War wounds,' was the cryptic response. 'It's nothing—a slight cut, that's all. I usually make a point of removing anything remotely fragile the instant we step on board. I guess I slipped up this time.'

'Even so, you may need a few stitches. Would you like me to take a look. . .?'

'*Morton*! Are you going to stand there gossiping all day while I die of neglect here?'

'Fat chance,' came the twinkling response.

'Perhaps I'd better take a look at her,' said Lindsey. 'See if I can find out what the problem is.'

'I'm not so sure that's a good idea.' There was a more serious note in the secretary's voice now. 'I'm used to her ways. It's not that she means. . .'

'*Morton*!'

'Oh, well,' the secretary shrugged, 'on your head be it—let's hope only metaphorically! Just be prepared to duck.' She led the way through to the nearby bedroom. 'Miss Duncan, the doctor's here.'

'Thank God!' The words were little more than a whisper.

Lindsey found herself gazing with fascination at the

figure reclining in the bed. Dressed, or rather undressed, in a satin nightdress, Adele Duncan lay with her eyes closed, one hand thrown dramatically across her face, her long dark hair tumbling over the pillows. A scene from one of her films could hardly have been more perfectly stage-managed, the thought hovered, traitorously, while Lindsey managed to subdue an instinct to applaud. She was, after all, a doctor, and the patient certainly looked highly flushed.

'Oh, Doctor, thank heaven you've come!' One delicate hand plucked fretfully at the sheet. 'I'm going to die. I just know I'm going to die, and no one cares.'

'I'm sure that isn't true, Miss Duncan,' Lindsey said gently. Setting her briefcase on a nearby table, she approached the bed. 'I'm certain a great many people care. *I* certainly do.'

The image of frailty was gone as heavily lashed eyes opened wide to glare accusingly in Lindsey's direction. 'Who are you? I asked for Dr Grant. *Morton!*'

'It isn't Miss Morton's fault,' Lindsey reasoned quietly. 'Dr Grant was making a round when your call came through to the hospital, and as I happened to be on duty. . .'

'I don't care who's on duty.' The American accent deepened. 'I want Niall. He's a friend, he understands my special needs. I have a very delicate disposition.'

'I'm sure you do, Miss Duncan.' Lindsey caught and averted her eyes swiftly from the silent laughter of Miss Morton. 'But surely that's all the more reason to act quickly? I understand you're experiencing some chest pain?' She reached for her stethoscope.

'You can put that thing away!' The actress's voice was becoming more strident, her cheeks more flushed,

Lindsey noted with a keen, professional gaze. It would be too easy to put everything down to a typical case of hysteria, but what if there was something else, some underlying cause? It was a risk she couldn't afford to take. In any case, she was a doctor, it was her job to treat patients, not to make assumptions.

'There can be any number of causes of chest pain,' Lindsey smiled reassuringly as she reached for the slender wrist. 'Are you taking any medication?' Her gaze rose questioningly to Miss Morton, who nodded silently in the direction of an array of small bottles that littered the bedside table.

'I refuse to discuss my medical history with anyone but Dr Grant. I'm sure if you tell him I need him, he'll be right here.'

'Quite right too.' The voice coming from behind her sent Lindsey whirling to face Niall, and she felt a ridiculous surge of relief run through her as he walked, smiling, into the cabin.

'Niall!' Tears sprang into Adele Duncan's eyes as she held out her hands. 'Oh, Niall, I just knew you'd come! I have such pain. My heart's beating so fast!'

Her own wasn't exactly dawdling either! Lindsey shunted the thought quickly aside, appalled to feel the faint colour rising in her cheeks as she forced herself to meet Niall's questioning gaze.

She deliberately lowered her voice as they moved fractionally away from the bed. 'I'm afraid I haven't been able to make a proper examination.' Why did she feel like a raw beginner in medical school, having to explain her actions, or rather her lack of them, to a senior? 'The pulse-rate is certainly fast. At this stage anything else would be pure guesswork. It could be any number of things. I'm sorry I wasn't able to do more. In the circumstances. . .'

'You did what you could. The circumstances are hardly usual.' A wry note entered the deep tones. 'Don't worry about it.' Niall's voice suddenly assumed a practical note as he turned to the occupant of the bed. 'Now let's see if we can find out exactly where this pain is and what's causing it, shall we?'

Feeling as if she had been dismissed, Lindsey watched as he sat on the bed and reached for his stethoscope.

'It's my heart.' Blue eyes filled with tears.

'Well, it certainly is beating a little fast. The question is, what's causing it?' smiled Niall. 'I'm sure Dr Blake will agree, there could be any number of reasons—isn't that so, Dr Blake?'

If I were wearing a next-to-nothing nightie and he was sitting on my bed, I'd be having serious trouble breathing too! The thought flitted quickly through Lindsey's mind.

'Indigestion?' she suggested mildly.

'Possibly.' Niall gave her a long searching look from which she purposely averted her gaze.

'She got a call from Morrie,' said Miss Morton.

They both turned to the secretary. 'Morrie?'

'Morrie Steinberg—Miss Duncan's agent.'

A faint cry of anguish came from the direction of the bed.

'I think perhaps you'd better explain,' Niall advised hardly.

'Miss Duncan's name was put forward for the possible lead in Arnie Costow's new production of *All the Fond Dreams*,' the secretary explained.

Niall's eyes widened appreciatively. 'I saw the stage version. I remember, it was impressive.'

'The screen version is already expected to break box-office records. Unfortunately Morrie phoned to say the lead had gone to Bonnie Grace.'

'*Bonnie Grace!*' Adele Duncan's hand fluttered to her eyes.

'A good choice, I'd have thought,' Niall stated evenly.

Lindsey stared at him in disbelief. The anguished cry became a wail. Miss Morton covered her face with her hands.

'I'm no expert, of course,' Niall contrived, apparently unperturbed. 'But I would have thought the role called for a mature lead. Now the part of the younger sister. . . Martha. . .?'

The wailing died away. Miss Morton peered through her spread fingers.

'Martha?' Adele Duncan raised herself from the pillows.

'Of course, I gather it's a pretty taxing role. Some say it's by far the more challenging of the two. I can't say I envy the director, having to find the right balance of youth and experience. . .' Niall broke off.

'Morton!'

'Yes, Miss Duncan?'

'Call Morrie,' ordered the actress.

'But it's the middle of the night where he. . .'

'I don't care if it's three in the morning! Get on the phone. Call him. If he's asleep, wake him.'

'Easy now,' Niall murmured soothingly. 'Remember the palpitations.'

A bejewelled hand stole out to cover his. 'Come to

New York, Niall,' begged Adele. 'You're wasted here, and I need you.'

It was easy to see why any man would be beguiled by the woman, Lindsey found herself thinking. She was beautiful, with an air of fragility which, for all she suspected it hid a character as hard as nails, yet was guaranteed to bring out the male protective instinct. And it certainly seemed to be working. The thought rose uncharitably to fill her mind, and suddenly, for some inexplicable reason, the sight of Adele Duncan's tearful smile and Niall's look of concern filled her with an emotion she refused to acknowledge as jealousy.

'Better to err on the side of caution, don't you think?'

She jerked back to the realisation that Niall was speaking. 'I. . . I'm sorry?' she queried.

His dark brows drew together. 'I was saying we can arrange to move Miss Duncan to the hospital for a while, just to make a few precautionary tests.'

In desperation Lindsey straightened up, reaching defensively for her briefcase. 'Yes, well. . .' Casting a fleeting smile at the woman in the bed, she moved towards the door. 'Clearly I'm not needed here. I'm already late for surgery, and I'm sure I can leave you safely in Dr Grant's very capable hands.'

With a brief smile in the other woman's direction, she fled, taking refuge in the consulting-room, where she closed her eyes and leaned against the closed door, breathing hard.

Suddenly she felt angry with herself for having let her emotions get out of control. Damn! Damn! Damn! Why on earth had she reacted like that? Running out was totally unprofessional, but she had acted purely on instinct. Better that, she thought resignedly, than making a complete fool of herself.

She started, straightening up as Jill tapped and popped her head round the door.

'Just thought I'd let you know everything's up to date. Medications are done, so Tony and I will be off as soon as surgery's finished, if that's all right with you?'

'Yes, of course it is,' Lindsey smiled as she put her briefcase on the desk. 'Have a good time.'

'Oh, we will! I'll catch up with you later, and thanks again.' Smiling her appreciation, Jill waved and was gone.

Jim Lewis was in his office studying an X-ray film, as Lindsey made her way to Reception, pausing to drop in a report.

'I thought you might want this. I think we'll play safe and get another set of X-rays done.'

'Right, I'll see to it first thing.' Grinning, Jim switched off the bright light and removed the film he had been studying. 'Looking forward to going ashore?'

'Too much to do.' Lindsey shook her head, smiling. 'You wouldn't believe how the paperwork mounts up in such a short time.'

'Wouldn't I just?' Swivelling round in his chair, he dropped a pile of X-rays and accompanying notes on to the desk beside him. 'I'm still working my way through this little lot.' He launched himself out of the chair to rescue a rapidly cooling cup of coffee, grimacing slightly in disgust as he indicated the pot. 'Help yourself, if you think you can face it. So, how did it go yesterday?'

'Yesterday?'

'Your first glimpse of Madeira?' A tiny grin played round his mouth as he shot a glance at her. 'What else?'

Lindsey felt the faint colour tinge her cheeks as she helped herself to coffee she didn't really want. 'It was fabulous! Everything everyone said it would be and more.' And much too unsettling!

'It's one of my favourite stop-overs every time. Did you manage to take afternoon tea on the terrace at Reids Hotel?'

She shook her head. 'Too much to see and not enough time.'

'Ah, well, never mind, there's always next time.'

Lindsey willed her hands to remain steady on the cup. If there *was* a next time. Suddenly she was beginning to find working in close proximity to Niall Grant much too disturbing for her own peace of mind.

'We missed you at dinner last night,' said Jim.

'Sorry about that, but I got a spate of cabin calls. Most of them late arrivals back on board, suffering from too much sun or too much of the local wine.'

'It happens every time,' Jim grinned. 'Look, I've not planned a day ashore this time. I've got some catching up to do as well, but I thought I might just grab an hour, maybe late this afternoon when everything's relatively quiet. Time to have a drink at one of the local tavernas, maybe.'

'It sounds nice,' Lindsey agreed.

'So why don't you come along? We don't need to go far. There are plenty of nice little bars within easy walking distance of the ship. It'll give you a chance to soak up at least a little of the atmosphere.'

She felt herself weakening. 'It does sound tempting.'

'So, what time are you off duty?' he asked.

'About three, until this evening's surgery. I'm covering for Jill until then.'

'Couldn't be better.'

She gave a wry laugh. 'You're a bad influence, you know that?'

Brown eyes twinkled. 'I'll see you at three,' said Jim.

'I shall look forward to it, and now I really do have to do some work.'

With a brief wave Lindsey hurried along the corridor towards the consulting-room, where she sat at the desk, taking several deep breaths to compose herself before calling for her first patient.

In fact, as on the previous day, most of the passengers had already begun going ashore early, determined not to miss a minute of the time they had before the ship sailed again that evening.

She managed, just, to stifle a tart response as a young woman came into the consulting-room and sat carefully in the chair. Lindsey didn't even need to ask what the problem was. It was all too evident in the red, blistered skin of her shoulders and arms.

'I didn't realise it was so hot,' came the inevitable cry of protest. 'We only stayed on the beach for a couple of hours or so, and there was a breeze.'

Lindsey almost flinched herself as she made a gentle examination of the blistered area. 'You realise, don't you, that it's highly dangerous to leave your skin exposed to sunlight without some kind of covering?'

'I just didn't think.'

Lindsey bit back a sigh of impatience. 'There are some excellent lotions and creams on the market these days. The higher the factor, the greater the protection.' She shook her head. 'Obviously it's a little late to prevent the damage now, but in future, remember, either cover up, or if you can't, stay out of the sun. Best of all, always use a screening lotion.'

'But it's only sunburn. It can't be dangerous,' protested the patient.

'It can be highly dangerous,' Lindsey insisted. 'Every year sees an increasing number of malignant melanomas — skin cancers — caused by exposure to direct sunlight. What I can do now is treat the damage and give you something to soothe the burning. But in future, remember.'

'Don't worry, I'm going straight to the chemist now to buy some sun-screen lotion.'

Seeing the girl out, Lindsey shook her head, wondering how much of her warning lecture would be heeded.

With a sigh she turned to the next patient, smiling as a young woman carried a small child into the room.

'Mrs Drew, what can I do for you?' Smiling, she reached out a hand towards the fretful infant. 'And who are you?'

'It's Daniel, Doctor. He just doesn't seem right. I think he's running a temperature, and he's off his food. His dad thought it might be the heat, but I'm not so sure.' The woman looked expectantly at Lindsey.

'Any vomiting? Headache?'

'No, but now you come to mention it, he has been coughing a bit.'

'Ah. Let's just have a listen to his chest, then, shall we?' Smiling, Lindsey leaned forward, stethoscope held to the chest of the tearful infant who sat, wide-eyed, on his mother's knee. 'Yes, well, he does sound a bit congested. No wonder the poor little chap is feeling a bit miserable!' She ruffled the child's hair and with a look of surprise suddenly produced a jelly-baby. 'Oh my, what do we have here? Well, look at that! Is this yours?'

With a loud hiccough the red-cheeked infant detached his thumb from his mouth and laughed as he held out his hand. 'More, more!'

A second jelly-baby appeared. 'Any more of this and I think we might end up regretting it!' Lindsey smiled at the mother. 'I'm sure he'll be just fine. I'll write you up a prescription for an antibiotic. Make sure he takes it three times a day. Stick to a light diet—not too many jelly-babies,' she laughed. 'Plenty of fluids, and if he isn't looking decidedly better in a couple of days, come back and we'll take another look, but I'm sure you don't need to worry.'

Having seen the reassured mother smilingly on her way, Lindsey switched off the computer and set about clearing her desk. She was scarcely aware of the tapping at the door until it opened and Niall came into the room. His face was impassive as he stood there. He didn't say a word, but the tension in him was almost tangible.

'I need to talk to you,' he said shortly.

Swallowing hard, Lindsey swept up a pile of papers from the desk and dropped them into her briefcase. 'I was just on my way to a meeting.'

'It can wait.'

To her consternation she saw him push the door to a close and felt the pulse drumming in her throat as the lethal blue stare narrowed.

She hadn't noticed before quite how dark his hair was, or that it curled slightly against his collar. He had discarded his jacket and the short sleeves of his shirt revealed strong arms, a sprinkling of dark hairs contrasting with the tanned skin. Small wonder children and female passengers regarded him with an almost breathless adoration, she found herself thinking. Looks like his should carry a health warning: Loving this man can seriously affect your heart.

She tried to meet his eyes and couldn't. 'I'm already late,' she protested defensively.

'This won't take long. You owe me an explanation, Dr Blake. I don't intend to leave here without it.'

She licked her dry lips. 'Explanation?'

His mouth tightened. 'You walked out, not only on me, but on a patient. I think I'm entitled to know why, don't you?'

CHAPTER NINE

ENTITLED, maybe, but Lindsey wasn't sure she could give an explanation. She would have liked to walk out right now, but Niall's tough, unyielding frame blocked her only means of escape. She was so powerfully aware of him that she could feel the ripples of panic beginning to spread.

Her mouth firmed mutinously. 'You seemed to be doing very well without my assistance. In any case, I wasn't aware that it was company policy for two doctors to attend a patient.'

For an instant she told herself she had imagined the almost feral glint behind the long, dark lashes as Niall said casually, 'If I didn't know better, I might almost get the idea that you were jealous.'

Her head jerked up. An odd smile tugged at the corners of his firm mouth. *Jealous!* She choked on the idea. To be jealous implied an involvement, a relationship, the very things she was fighting against. In any case, the mere word was anathema to her, she thought fiercely. It was Paul's obsessive jealousy which had diseased and finally destroyed her feelings for him, even though it was an emotion she had never fully understood — until now.

Niall's half-closed eyes glinted. 'But of course, that would be crazy, wouldn't it?' he drawled softly, and lightly kissed her trembling mouth.

Colour rioted into her cheeks. 'Be careful, Dr Grant! Your ego is showing.'

'I'm a doctor.' His voice was even and dispassionate. 'It's my job to offer reassurance, if that's what's required, as well as medical treatment. You of all people should know that.'

And if anyone could bottle that particular type of reassurance it would make a million overnight, the thought flitted inconsequentially into her mind.

She bit her lip, knowing that the core of his argument was true. She was doubly on the defensive as his gaze flicked over her, taking in the pale lemon dress she was wearing, its scooped neckline, she suddenly realised, revealing the deepening suntan on her shoulders and the curve of her breasts.

'Alcohol doesn't solve problems,' she stated flatly.

'True, it may not solve them. Adele obviously uses it as some kind of defence. I'm not saying I condone it,' he interpreted her look, 'but at the moment maybe it's all she has to protect her from feelings of inadequacy.'

'Inadequacy!' Lindsey couldn't prevent the sharp laugh of incredulity. 'Adele Duncan has everything most people spend a lifetime dreaming about!'

'Appearances can be deceptive. It may not be obvious to everyone, but beneath that ice-cool exterior, Adele is a deeply unhappy lady.'

'Maybe there's such a thing as having too much of a good thing,' she flung at him caustically.

Niall's gaze narrowed. 'She hasn't made a film in five years.'

Her frowning gaze met his. '*Midnight Stranger* — I remember it. Was it really five years ago? Didn't it win her an Oscar or something?'

'Won her an Oscar, lost her a husband.'

The look she flung at him now was one of incredulity. 'You're not serious?'

'It isn't widely known,' Niall advised drily. 'He vanished, along with some up-and-coming young starlet. They were killed. Apparently the private jet they were travelling in crashed into the side of a mountain in thick fog.'

'I had no idea,' Lindsey said. 'How awful!'

'I don't think she ever quite got over it. It's one reason why she always insists on travelling by ship rather than flying. Maybe it's a kind of therapy, who knows?'

'Maybe she'll meet someone else,' she floundered helplessly, realising she was on dangerous ground. The circumstances surrounding Adele Duncan's personal tragedy were so similar, how could Niall fail to be reminded of his own marriage break-up?

'Maybe she will.' His mouth curved into an ironic smile.

Maybe she already had! Lindsey gave a shaky laugh as he moved closer. Her gaze was drawn to the firm lines of his sensuous mouth, the lean-muscled body forcing her to a recognition of his powerful masculinity.

'You'd have to be a romantic to believe it,' he said slowly.

'Or less of a cynic,' she smiled, her voice sounding oddly husky. She saw him tense, heard the soft intake of his breath, then watched, fascinated, as he bent his head, brushing his lips against her mouth.

But he didn't stop there. Even as she was thinking about rallying her defences, his expression changed.

'Maybe we'd better find out just how much of a romantic you are, Dr Blake.'

Before she could offer a word in response, he had tilted her head back. He raised his head long enough to look at her, a question glittering in the blue eyes, and she answered it breathlessly, raising her eyes to his.

'This is crazy,' Niall muttered harshly before his mouth took possession of hers.

He was right, she thought. It was, utterly crazy, totally without logic. But at this moment she didn't care. She moaned as his mouth covered hers, sending a surge of pure physical awareness coursing through her.

Desire licked like a flame at her senses, sending dangerous signals to her brain. Crazy, crazy. But her fingers ran over the strong column of his neck, tangled in the dark silkiness of her hair at his nape, then he was drawing her soft, pliant curves closer until their bodies merged in a powerful force of energy that was frightening, all-consuming in its intensity.

She should fight it, she knew. Her hands tensed against the solid wall of his chest, feeling the warm, muscular tautness of him. It wasn't him she wanted to run from, it was herself! To go on would be like stepping blindfold into the dark, and she wasn't ready.

She closed her eyes as, with slow deliberation, Niall drew her back into his arms. Weakly she willed him not to, but if he sensed her resistance he ignored it, his mouth tantalising her with its warm desirability.

Lindsey knew she had been fooling herself in thinking she could remain indifferent. His kiss was betraying her into feelings she would have rather have held back. There was no possible future in this.

'Please, no,' she protested weakly, and heard him groan softly.

'Lindsey, I need you. You must know how much I want you,' he rasped, cupping her face, drawing her inexorably back to invade again the full softness of her mouth.

Her senses felt drugged. Oh, it was so unfair! She stiffened in his arms, saw the turmoil in his eyes and panicked as she sensed how little it would take to make her surrender. If he kissed her again. . . Her hands pushed against his chest.

'No, I don't think this is such a good idea.'

He released her abruptly, breathing hard. 'Lindsey, what is it? You know I wouldn't do anything to hurt you.'

Not knowingly, maybe. She shook her head, still trembling as she pressed a hand to her mouth. 'Neither of us is thinking rationally,' she said bleakly. 'We have a good working relationship; let's just keep it at that, shall we? It'll be easier all round.' And far safer.

She saw him tense. A nerve pulsed in his jaw, then he let her go.

'If that's what you want.'

It wasn't, but how could she tell him that what she wanted was much, much more than he was prepared to give?

'Ready to go, my lovely?' Jim appeared, dressed in shorts and an outrageous T-shirt that had Lindsey in fits of laughter as she shed her white coat.

'With you in two minutes.'

'I thought a quick gallop, a guzzle of the local tincture and a few snaps to record the event for posterity.'

'You make it sound like the D-day landing!' she laughed.

'No point in hanging around, *cariad*. If you've only got a couple of hours, best make the most of them.'

Lindsey shook her head, smiling, as Jill came in. 'I've done the report book,' she explained. 'Everything's up to date. It's been pretty quiet, so you needn't have worried about hurrying back.'

'That's OK.' Jill slipped a pen into the pocket of her white dress. 'We've done all we needed to do, spent a heck of a lot more than we'd planned.' She grinned. 'Now it's your turn. Go and enjoy yourself.'

'I aim to see that she does, gorgeous,' Jim assured her.

'And you behave yourself.'

Jim assumed a look of mock innocence. 'Oh, ye of little faith, casting nasturtiums at my character!'

'You're incorrigible! Just go.' Jill pointed, laughing, at the door, and Jim playfully ushered Lindsey out as a pencil sailed past his ear. Minutes later the two of them were heading down the gangway.

Tenerife was basking in afternoon sunshine as a taxi dropped them off at the sea-front. In a temperature of nearly ninety degrees, Lindsey was glad she had thought to bring a hat with her as they strolled along the palm-strewn promenade, stopping at one of the many bars to drink a refreshingly cold iced lemonade.

Resuming their walk, she was surprised to discover that there was no sand. 'I expected to see a beach!' she exclaimed.

'Not in this part of the island,' Jim explained. 'It's all rock along this area of the coast. That's why the local authorities built the Lido. A lot of the tourists go over to the other side of the island, but I'm afraid we'll have to save that for another trip when we have more time.'

But it was beautiful for all that, Lindsey decided, leaning against a wall to stare out to sea. There was something exciting about the ruggedness of the coastline which offered such a sharp contrast to the many flowers and exotic plant life of the island.

'Oh, look, a market! Come on, let's explore.'

Jim threw up his hands in mock horror. 'Why is it that women can't resist shopping? Don't you get enough of it at home?'

'This is different,' Lindsey laughingly dismissed his protest, weaving her way with almost childlike excitement between rows of fruit and vegetables and racks of brightly coloured sundresses, sandals and locally made lace.

Unable to resist, she decided to treat herself to one of the dresses in a shade of pale coral. She was paying for it when her eye was caught by a stall covered with delicately made tablecloths and other handmade items.

To her delight she discovered the perfect wedding present, a set of sheets and matching pillowcases, all edged with lace and stitched with rosebuds. 'I'll take them,' she said decisively, not even bothering to haggle over the price, knowing that she couldn't have found anything even remotely comparable at home. And they would always be a perfect reminder, she told herself as they finally struggled back on board, loaded with parcels, none of which she had actually intended to buy.

Jim was right; the break had done her good. Her cabin, when she returned to it, was beautifully cool, and she headed for the shower, stripping off her clothes as she went. With another full evening of entertainment ahead, many of the passengers were probably doing the same, she realised, relishing the needle-sharp tingling of the water as it cascaded over her shoulders.

And now for a cup of tea, she thought, stepping out to wind a large bath towel around her nakedness. But no sooner had she switched on the electric kettle than the phone began to ring. With a resigned sigh she went to answer it.

'Thank God! Where the hell have you been?' demanded Niall's controlled but definitely angry voice. 'I've been trying to get hold of you for the past half-hour!'

Her eyes flared with shock and resentment. How dared he? With an effort she managed to keep her voice calm. 'I've been ashore, enjoying a short break to which I was perfectly entitled,' she flung back at him. 'I wasn't aware I needed your permission.'

There was a momentary silence during which she could imagine him rallying for another attack. For a moment she thought he was going to slam the phone down, then she heard him give a deep sigh.

'I'm sorry—I over-reacted. I'm afraid we have an emergency, and it's not something I can handle alone. I'm going to need your help, Lindsey, *now*.'

She sat heavily on the bed. Something in his voice seemed to penetrate her brain, having a calming effect. 'What's happened?' she asked.

'It's Mrs Walker.'

'Walker.' She frowned. 'Alison Walker. Seven months preg. . .' She felt her stomach tighten. 'Not the baby? She's not in labour?'

'I wish to God it were that simple. Look, can you get

down here? I think we may have to move fast. I'll fill you in on the details then.'

'I'll be there. Give me five minutes.' As Niall rang off Lindsey was already reaching for her clothes.

She made it in four, her hair still wet from the shower, wearing jeans and a T-shirt beneath the white coat she had hastily thrown on.

'What's the problem?' she asked briskly as she walked into the room.

Niall glanced up from the desk. 'She presented with abdominal pain and bleeding about an hour ago.'

Lindsey drew in a breath. 'Severe?'

He shook his head. 'No, but sustained. Apparently it began some time last night.'

'And she didn't do anything about it?'

'Apparently she thought it might just go away.'

'Hoped it might,' Lindsey retorted. 'Either way, at this stage, in the third trimester, it isn't good. Could it be appendicitis?'

He frowned. 'It's a possibility. Ideally I would have liked a scan. I'm not convinced about the appendicitis — the symptoms don't quite add up.'

Lindsey's mouth tightened. 'Placenta praevia?'

'I don't think so. There's no history of previous Caesarian section or induced abortion.' Niall shook his head. 'I'm more inclined to opt for placental abruption. The trouble is, I'm guessing.'

Lindsey's gaze met his. 'What about the baby?'

'So far it's fine, but there's definite foetal distress. The heartbeat is depressed.' He glanced at his watch. 'Fifteen minutes ago it was low to normal at eighty.'

Lindsey drew in a sharp breath. 'It should be between

a hundred and twenty and a hundred and forty. Have you done an internal examination?'

'No, it's too risky. If there's any chance it is placenta praevia, it could detach and cause a haemorrhage. That's why we have to make a decision and act now.'

'So what do we do?' she asked.

'We don't have any choice,' said Niall with a calm she envied. 'If we simply sit back and do nothing, we could lose both mother and baby. We have to operate and if necessary do a Caesarian section.' As if he sensed the turmoil she was feeling, he reached out to rest his hands on her shoulders. 'Don't worry, you'll be fine.' His mouth twisted slightly. 'How are you at anaesthetics?'

She managed a shaky grin. 'Actually, pretty good.' She looked at him. 'Have you told her yet?'

'No.' He ran a hand through his hair. 'Theatre's on alert. I needed to study the report. I thought we'd go and have a chat with her now.'

Alison Walker lay pale-faced and tearful, one hand instinctively resting over her swollen abdomen as if to protect the child within. She gave a slight sob as they came towards her, her eyes wide with fear.

'My baby. . . He's going to be all right, isn't he? I'm not going to lose him, not now?'

Lindsey quickly took the other woman's hand in hers. 'He's fine, so far. There is a problem, but we're going to do something about it. You and the baby are both going to be all right.' She shot a look at Niall. 'Aren't they?'

He looked at her and she felt the colour rising in her cheeks at the knowledge that she was breaking one of the first rules of medicine, which was never to make promises you couldn't possibly guarantee to keep. But if he was aware of it, there was certainly no sign as he said very quietly, 'Yes, of course they are.'

She swallowed hard, fighting for composure. Maybe she couldn't offer guarantees, but somehow she knew that if anyone could save this baby, Niall was that person.

She watched and listened as he sat on the bed, held the frightened woman's hand and made her believe it too.

'What we think is happening,' he explained quietly and unemotionally, 'is that the placenta which carries the blood supply to your baby is beginning to detach itself and break up. Obviously we don't want that to happen. Ideally your baby isn't quite ready to be born.' He smiled. 'But it seems this particular young man is in something of a hurry. Perhaps he wants to enjoy the cruise too.'

Alison Walker's mouth quivered on a tearful smile. 'So. . .what can you do?'

'First of all, I'd like to examine you. My hands are warm,' Niall joked, 'and I promise I'll try not to hurt you.'

Lindsey watched, fascinated, as the strong hands moved with surprising gentleness. Even so, Alison winced slightly, confirming their suspicion that the uterus was tender and contracted.

Niall straightened up immediately, rearranging the sheet. 'That's fine. So what we want to do now is carry out a Caesarian section and help this young chap into the world before he runs into any real trouble. It's quite a straightforward operation, and we have all the necessary facilities to perform it.'

Alison Walker's face was white, but she managed to smile. 'Yes, I know. Dr Blake got one of the nurses to show me.' She gave a jerky laugh. 'I didn't think I'd actually need them!'

'Well, at least now you can put your mind at rest and leave the rest to us. Sister will be in shortly to get you ready. We'll send you off to sleep, and when you wake up it will all be over.'

He made it sound so simple, Lindsey found herself thinking, as finally they moved away from the bed. Because of her training, she knew the risks involved, not only to the mother but in delivering a live, healthy baby. Yet somehow she shared Alison Walker's faith that everything would be all right.

Lindsey could feel the tiny rivulets of sweat running down her back beneath the green operating gown as she kept her gaze fixed firmly on the monitors.

'How is she doing at your end?' Niall's voice, slightly muffled by the mask, broke calmly into the silence.

'Fine.'

'Keep up the good work. Let me know instantly if there's any change. I want this over with as quickly as possible. Suction here.' She heard his sharp intake of breath. 'Right, out you come, young fellow. Now!'

Lindsey saw his expression change and suddenly, amazingly, he held the squirming scrap of life in his hands. She drew a breath as he gazed at it for an instant, watching its slow movements, the gentle opening of its tiny mouth as if expressing surprise. 'Well, hello, baby Walker. Welcome to the world!'

Watching him, Lindsey could have sworn she saw a sudden brightness in his eyes before he was handing the infant over. 'Here we go, little chap. I still have work to do.'

Tess Milner, the senior theatre sister, moved in, taking the baby and wrapping him in a blanket, leaving Niall free to attend to the unconscious woman. She laughed. 'Well, look at that! He's sucking his thumb!'

There was an instant relieving of the tension as everyone joined in the laughter. Lindsey looked up to find Niall watching her, his expression telling her that he understood and shared at least some part of what she was feeling.

After that, it was a matter of routine procedure. An hour later, mother and baby were sleeping peacefully, and Lindsey emerged, having shed her mask and gown to draw in some deep breaths as she stepped into the welcome fresh air.

She felt drained, both physically and mentally, yet at the same time strangely exhilarated. For the first time she could sense what it must be like to possess the surgeon's power almost of life and death, the satisfaction of knowing your actions had helped to save a life or bring a new one into the world, and she had been a part, albeit a small one, of the drama.

It came as a shock to discover, when she stepped outside, that it was dark. The last time she had seen Niall he had been checking on his patients.

Somehow she seemed to have lost track of time. The ship was filled with light and sound. In an hour they would be sailing again and most of the passengers, having dined, would now be watching one of the cabarets.

A sound caused her to jump slightly and she half turned to see a figure silhouetted in the doorway. She didn't need to see his face to know it was Niall. As he came towards her out of the darkness the inevitable shock of physical awareness swept over her, sharpened now by the experience they had just shared.

'I had an idea I might find you out here.'

Shivering slightly, she managed to look at him and smile. 'I couldn't face the noise,' she explained. 'I needed a bit of space to unwind and think.'

'I know the feeling.' He came to stand beside her, close but not touching.

She blinked a sudden and totally illogical misting of tears from her eyes. 'How are the patients?' she asked.

'Mother and baby both doing fine. The little one's a bit on the small side. He'll need to be in an incubator for a while, just as a precautionary measure. I've arranged to have them transferred ashore to the local hospital. They can be flown home from there.'

'I'm glad.' Her voice came out thickly. 'If you hadn't taken the decision, done what you did. . .'

'Hey!' His hands were on her shoulders, turning her gently to face him. 'This wasn't a one-man show, you were as much a part of it as I was. It was a team effort.'

It was true. It was a long time since Lindsey had experienced such a feeling of fulfilment. She enjoyed the experience, the challenge of working with Niall. But where was it leading? the thought came home sharply to her. There was no possible future in it.

She shivered as tiredness and reaction set in. Her life had seemed so settled, so straightforward, until this man had come along to complicate it.

Without being aware of it she sighed, and became the subject of Niall's intense scrutiny. His eyes were dark as he looked at her.

'Lindsey, what's wrong?'

She shrugged. 'I know it's crazy, but I've only just begun to realise how much I'm going to miss all this.' She turned away, only to have him take hold of her arm, forcing her to look at him.

'What the hell are you saying?' he demanded. 'Why should you miss it?'

'You've obviously forgotten,' she said, trying to keep control of her voice. 'I'm a probationer. My contract runs out at the end of this trip. It's back to good old Civvy Street and more sociable hours.'

His grip on her arms tightened, making her wince. 'It would simply be a formality to renew it on a long-term basis.'

Lindsey closed her eyes, wishing him a million miles away. It didn't work. When she opened them again Niall was still there, still a threat. She would need to be a masochist to put herself through this kind of torment, seeing him every day, working with him, knowing it could never lead anywhere.

She forced a smile, deciding that flippancy was her only defence. 'You'd be surprised how quickly the prospect of a nine-to-five job can take on a certain charm!'

'I hadn't realised your ambitions were quite so basic or mercenary,' said Niall drily.

'They're not,' she said. Oh, why was he making this so difficult? Her chin rose. 'If you must know, I. . . I've been offered a job in general practice. My uncle is looking for someone to replace a partner who's retiring.' Mentally she crossed her fingers on the lie. It was true, Uncle Max had said many times that if she decided to take up general practice he'd be only too happy to have her join him, but that wasn't quite the same thing as actually being offered a job.

'So that's it!' His gaze narrowed. 'You're a damn good doctor. I thought you enjoyed your work.'

'I do.'

'So why follow the herd?' His hands were biting into her flesh. 'At least think about it. Why throw away the chance to do something different?' he persisted.

Because it was safe, she thought. Because he only had to be in the same room for her nervous system to run haywire, and she could only take so much punishment.

It needed an effort, but she managed to smile back at him. 'I seem to recall hearing you say that the last thing you needed was a husband-hunting female who thinks this is some sort of pleasure cruise. Are you actually asking me to stay?'

His response caught her completely unawares. 'I can't make that decision for you,' he said raggedly. 'I don't have that right.'

But she was giving him that right, she felt like shouting. All he had to do was say the words. But then that was the problem. He might want her as a doctor, but as a woman, it seemed, she was a disposable commodity.

She managed to free herself, stepping back to breathe in deeply. 'I'll think about it,' she said lightly.

'When do you have to let your uncle have a decision?'

'Soon.' Lindsey wondered at her ability to lie so easily. 'Obviously if I decide not to take the job he'll need to start looking for a replacement.' And if she decided not to renew her contract she would soon be joining the ranks of the unemployed. Not that she imagined she would have any difficulty finding a job. It was just that nothing would ever seem quite the same again.

'Lindsey.'

She hesitated at the door.

'We'll be in Greece in forty-eight hours. Come ashore with me—I have a few things I must do. It seems a shame to waste the opportunity to see something of the country.'

It was on the tip of tongue to refuse, then she stifled a sigh. After all, why not? It was true, Greece was one place she had always wanted to see, and what had she to lose?

'All right,' she said. It was as if an uneasy truce had been called. So why did she get the feeling that she hadn't won the battle, but merely postponed the war?

CHAPTER TEN

'A CAR!' Stepping ashore from the small tender that ferried passengers to and from the ship, Lindsey found herself being led towards the vehicle parked nearby. 'You mean this is yours?'

'Not exactly.' Niall handed her in before moving round to ease his own lean height in behind the wheel. 'I have an arrangement with the local hire company. They know when the ship is due in and arrange to have a vehicle waiting for me when we land.' His mouth twisted slightly as he found the ignition and they set off, leaving behind a trail of smoke. 'I have to admit, this isn't the usual model.'

'Where exactly are we going?' Lindsey asked.

'Some friends of mine live a few kilometres from here. I try to see them as often as I can. It's been some time.' Niall glanced in the rear-view mirror. 'I thought you'd enjoy meeting some of the local people, away from the usual tourist traps. Nikos and Maria will give us lunch.'

'I'm ashamed to say I've never eaten Greek food before,' she told him.

He took his gaze briefly from the road to flick a smile briefly in her direction. 'You'll enjoy it.'

Lindsey was prepared to take his word for it as she settled back, content to drink in the spectacularly breathtaking scenery.

For the past two days she had been dreading the

160

proximity this trip would involve, but gradually, as the car wound its way along the narrow mountain roads, she could feel herself beginning to relax.

The early morning sun was already gathering heat as they left the ship behind, anchored in the now-distant bay below, and she was glad she had chosen to wear the thin jade silk blouse with her white jeans. Even so, she shifted uncomfortably as a tiny rivulet of sweat ran between her shoulderblades.

'I'm glad you had the sense to bring a hat.' Niall glanced at the white baseball-type cap lying on her knees.

'It was all I could find — courtesy of Jim, actually,' Lindsey admitted wryly.

His eyes glinted. 'I'm sure it will do far more for you. Anyway, it doesn't matter what you wear as long as you wear something. You're not used to this heat. It's cool yet compared to what it will be in a couple of hours' time.'

'Cool!' She fanned herself with the hat. Even the breeze lifting the honeyed hair from her neck was hot. 'It must be ninety degrees already!'

Glancing from beneath her lashes, Lindsey studied his profile, and found it unnerving, or perhaps it was simply that the confining space of the small car didn't allow much distance between driver and passenger.

Flushing slightly, she rested her head back and closed her eyes, not to sleep, but with the deliberate intention of shutting him from her mind.

Some time later he manoeuvred a tight bend and, caught unawares, she slid towards him, her body making solid contact with the muscular tautness of his thigh. He was hard and warm, and the faint musky tang of his aftershave teased her nostrils, evoking memories she would far rather had lain dormant. Flushing hotly, she sat up rigidly, bracing herself in the seat.

'Sorry,' she muttered.

'I should have warned you,' said Niall. 'The roads get worse the higher we climb. Go back to sleep — you must be exhausted.'

It didn't seem to be affecting him, she noticed. He still managed to look cool in the denims and white sweatshirt.

'I was just resting my eyes.'

His eyes met hers and there was a slight movement at the corners of his mouth. 'You slept for about half an hour,' he told her.

'Oh. It must be the heat.'

'Don't worry about it, your head on my shoulder was no weight at all.'

Lindsey turned away quickly, staring in confusion at a scene which was breathtakingly beautiful and which, she knew already, would stay imprinted on her mind for ever.

'Even the light seems different,' she murmured, forgetting her embarrassment as the car climbed steadily along the road twisting between spectacular mountains and valleys hung about by a still blue haze.

'I suppose it must be a combination of the sea and the heat. I've never seen anything quite like it anywhere in the world.' Niall manoeuvred a particularly tight bend which had Lindsey gripping the edges of her seat as they seemed only inches away from a sheer drop. He nodded casually in the direction of the tree-strewn hills all around them. 'Those are olives, and down there, in the valley, you can see the almond orchards.'

'I can't believe I'm actually seeing all this!' She turned to smile at him. 'Why do I get the feeling that nothing much has changed since. . .oh, I don't know, Biblical times.'

'Probably because it hasn't. Olive trees can grow to be well over a thousand years old.' The corners of his mouth twitched. 'It tends to make you look at things from a whole new perspective, don't you think?'

Lindsey sank back into her seat, trying to digest the thought that that was precisely what she had been trying to do from the minute she had met him, and it hadn't got her very far.

'Just where do these friends of yours live?' she rallied, deliberately injecting a note of brightness into her voice. 'Are you sure they won't mind having a total stranger thrust upon them without as much as a by your leave?'

Niall looked amused. 'It's not far. As for Nikos and Maria, they'll be only too delighted. Not simply because they happen to run one of the best tavernas in the region, but because they've always issued a standing invitation for me to bring anyone I care to.'

'Have you known them long?' Lindsey asked.

'I met them on one of my early trips out here.'

Which meant he must have brought Claire up here. Even though she knew it was illogical, the thought briefly took the edge off her enjoyment.

A tiny knot of tension throbbed at the back of her neck, running the length of her arms to her fingertips. She deliberately relaxed her limbs, looking steadily out of the open window, inhaling deeply as she tried to pinpoint an elusive scent. 'What's that lovely smell?'

'Probably a combination of almond blossom and

lemon trees.' Niall took his eyes from the road long
enough to glance in her direction. 'Have you ever been
to Delphi?'

'No, I haven't.'

'According to the ancient Greeks, when Zeus wanted
to find the centre of the earth, he released one eagle to
fly eastwards and another westwards. The two birds
met at Delphi and sat on a stone, the navel of the
earth.' There was a slight movement at the corners of
his mouth. 'Of course, he might not be geographically
correct, but it makes a good story.'

Lindsey sighed for sheer joy and wonderment. 'It's
all so beautiful and. . .unreal. How do you know where
the legend ends and reality begins?'

He laughed. 'You don't. Just go with it, it's easier.'
He glanced at his watch. 'We're almost there.'

Lindsey sat up as the car swept round yet another
bend, running gradually to a flatter, fertile coastal plain.
Suddenly the road grew wider and the trees were left
behind as they reached a small town of almost glaringly
white buildings set against a backdrop of hills and
fronted by a tiny harbour.

Lindsey barely had time to catch a glimpse of colourful awnings and flower-filled terracotta pots before Niall
had brought the car to a halt, cut the engine and was
climbing out.

The gate to a tiny courtyard was open and, for an
instant, Lindsey hung back, watching in rapt fascination
as a dark-haired, slender figure came hurrying down
the steps towards them, cloth in hand, and flung herself
into Niall's arms.

'Niall! *Ti kanete*?' In her excitement, switching from

Greek to broken English, she held him at arm's length
before kissing him soundly on both cheeks.

Laughing, Niall swept her effortlessly from her feet,
returning the kiss measure for measure, and Lindsey
had to look away as jealousy seared through her like a
forest fire out of control.

She stood motionless, waiting for the two to break
apart, and found herself staring at the girl from whom
Niall was now gently detaching himself.

'Nikos!' she called, gesturing excitedly, waving the
cloth as a head appeared at an upper window. There
followed a torrent of Greek, of which Lindsey understood only the word 'Niall', before she tucked one
slender hand through his arm.

She was certainly lovely, Lindsey had to admit.
Typically Greek, she had long dark hair swept back and
tied with a ribbon. Beneath a brightly coloured apron
she wore a full cotton skirt and short-sleeved, scooped-
neck blouse. Smiling brown eyes looked perceptively in
Lindsey's direction.

'Maria, I'd like you to meet Lindsey—Dr Blake.'

'*Despinis*. . . Dr Blake,' came the shy response. 'We
are so pleased to welcome you to our home.'

'Please call me Lindsey.'

'Eh, Nikos!' Smiling, Maria chivvied the dark-haired
young man who came to grasp Niall's hand and was
slapping his shoulder. 'This is Dr. . .is Lindsey, a friend
of Niall's.'

'*Kalimera*,' Lindsey attempted shyly. '*Chero poli*?
How do you do?'

'It's been a long time, my friend.'

'Too long,' Niall agreed.

Nikos smiled and said something softly in Greek, and

for some reason Lindsey found herself blushing at the sudden contact of Niall's hand against her arm, but she couldn't interpret the look he gave her as they were ushered towards one of the few empty tables overlooking the harbour.

'Come,' Maria insisted, 'be comfortable. You must be hot and thirsty.'

Within seconds the brightly coloured cloth had been whipped away, to be replaced by a fresh one. Glasses appeared and a bottle of wine. 'Or maybe you like the fresh lemonade?'

'I'd love it,' Lindsey smiled gratefully.

'How long you stay?' Nikos turned to say goodbye to some customers, flapped a cloth over the table he had emptied before turning his gaze back to Niall.

'A couple of hours, maybe,' announced Niall. 'We have to be back for evening surgery.'

Disappointment briefly etched their faces. 'So, you eat now,' Maria insisted. 'We eat and talk.' And in no time at all, it seemed, plates of food arrived — a delicious mixture of fish, most of which Lindsey dismally failed to recognise.

'Is a local dish,' Maria explained shyly. 'Is. . . xyphios.' She pointed to the delicately grilled squares arranged on skewers. 'How you say. . .swordfish, with the sauce of tomato, onion and the bayleaf. Is good, no?'

'It's very good, yes,' Lindsey agreed, laughing.

The four of them sat in the sun, Lindsey mostly listening, but happily so, sipping at her lemonade. The ship seemed a million light years away as she tilted her head back, letting the liquid slide coolly down her throat.

Almost involuntarily she sighed, her arm out-stretched along the back of the wooden seat.

'Have some more. It's sensible to increase your liquid intake in this heat.' Niall handed her a refilled glass, his glance travelling over her soft curves.

Her body reacted as if he had touched her, her breasts peaking with taut urgency. Her lashes swept down to feather her cheeks. He had only to look at her for all her firmly made resolutions to begin to melt away.

Her mind closed against the thought. She pushed back the warm honeyed tendrils of her hair from her neck, allowing a tantalising breeze to fan her skin.

Gradually, as most of the taverna's customers had drifted away, they carried their cups of the sweet Greek coffee into the more shaded area of a stone-paved terrace. Nikos and Niall strolled away, laughing together.

Maria smiled shyly as Lindsey lowered herself into one of the white chairs.

'Is a pity you cannot be here to meet Georgi.'

'Georgi?' queried Lindsey.

'Our son. He is at school. He will be sad to miss Niall—they are very close.' Maria's smile faded briefly. 'We owe Niall very much.'

'Oh?'

The smile returned. 'Georgi went with his papa to the market. He was very small then, five. . .maybe six. A baby still. So excited!' Maria lifted her hands and let them fall. 'Nikos is busy buying the vegetables and Georgi. . .ah, in a flash he is gone!' She looked up, smiling, as the men returned and Nikos sat with his arm draped around his wife's shoulders. 'I tell how Niall saved Georgi,' she explained.

Lindsey's gaze flew up to meet Niall's, and he shrugged dismissively. 'I just happened to be in the right place at the right time.'

'It could have been tragedy.' Nikos didn't share his humour. 'Georgi was too busy getting himself lost, he didn't see the lorry. It was a miracle only his leg was broken. If Niall hadn't been there, who knows what happen?'

'We are grateful always for what he did,' Maria said softly. 'Grateful to be given such a friend.'

'Hey, so we celebrate!' They all laughed as Nikos relieved the momentary tension by producing another bottle of wine and proceeded to fill fresh glasses. 'So, you and Niall are old friends, yes?'

'Actually, no,' Lindsey said casually. 'I only joined the ship at the beginning of this trip.'

'Ah. Is great adventure to go round the world, yes?'

She was heart-stoppingly aware of Niall watching her from the doorway, a glimmer of something she couldn't fathom in his blue eyes.

'Unfortunately, Dr Blake has other plans. Isn't that right?'

Lindsey's breath snagged in her throat. Why was he making it seem as if it was her fault, her choice? After all, she was the one who stood to lose most. How could she go on working with him, living so close to him, knowing that, deep down, he still loved Claire?

'Yes, I'm afraid it is. Some of us prefer to keep our feet on solid ground,' she added with a deliberately contrived laugh.

Despite the fact that she had been deeply touched by

the open friendliness of the Greek couple, it came almost as a relief when finally Niall signalled that it was time to leave.

'Maybe you come again.' Nikos kissed Lindsey soundly on the cheek.

Maria smiled before kissing her, too. 'You are always welcome.'

They were making it difficult for her to tear herself away. 'We have to go.' Niall's hand touched her shoulder and he must have been aware of her stiffening. He released her at once, and Lindsey felt a confusing ache somewhere deep inside her as they finally drove away.

'Glad you came?' he asked.

'Oh, yes.' She sent him a faint answering smile, because it was true. Even when he was no longer a part of her life, at least she would have her memories. 'Nikos and Maria are a lovely couple. They seem so happy together.'

'They've been besotted with each other more or less since they were children. It's pretty rare these days to find that sort of commitment.'

Had she imagined the slight edge to his voice? Lindsey wondered. If he was thinking of himself and Claire his expression told her nothing. Sighing, she turned to stare out of the window. If only her own emotions were so easily controlled!

It should have been cooler in the hills, but if anything, Lindsey thought drowsily, the heat was becoming even more intense with barely a breeze to relieve it. She was fanning her cheeks desultorily when she realised with a start that they were pulling off the road and Niall was bringing the car to a halt.

'What's wrong?' She sat bolt upright. 'Why are we stopping?'

Niall's frowning blue gaze ran over her before he pushed the door open and climbed out. 'The engine's overheating. It's hardly surprising after a climb like that.' He released a catch, springing open the bonnet, and twisted a metal cap, stepping back as it made a loud hissing sound.

Lindsey climbed out after him, staring in dismay at the escaping column of steam. 'Can you fix it?' she asked.

Using his handkerchief, he released the cap still further, increasing the jet of steam. 'It needs a chance to cool off and a spot of water.' Suddenly he looked tired, and there were deep furrows in his brow as his eyes scanned her for an instant. 'There are some cans of drink on the back seat if you're thirsty. Help yourself.'

She stared at him, noting the dark patches darkening his shirt, and became uncomfortably aware of the trickle of sweat running down her own back.

Handing him one of the cans, she drank from her own, and coughed as it went down the wrong way. It was removed instantly from her grasp.

'Take it more slowly,' ordered Niall. 'There's no need to panic. We're not stranded miles from civilisation. You're perfectly safe.'

'I'm not panicking!' Her voice sounded strained as the irony of his words hit her full force. Of course she was safe as long as she didn't weaken. The question was, was that really what she wanted?

He surveyed her in silence, his eyes narrowing on her

face, then, with a ragged sigh, he reached out and drew her roughly towards him.

'I've been telling myself I wouldn't let this happen,' he rasped, 'but there's something about you that drives me to the edge of my control.'

Lindsey swayed slightly as his mouth hovered, a breath away. What was she doing? He bent his head to brush a kiss against her faintly protesting lips, the slight shift of her body closing the infinitesimal barrier between them. She heard the soft intake of his breath, then he was drawing her down on to the grass.

His body was hard and warm; the faint citrus tang of his aftershave filled her nostrils. She breathed deeply, like a swimmer suddenly out of her depth, then his arms locked around her, crushing her against the tautly muscled wall of his chest.

For a brief moment, as she battled with the last remaining shreds of her resistance, Lindsey could feel the thud of his heartbeat, then excitement exploded, heady and intoxicating, as her hands relaxed against the warmth of his chest. If today was all she was allowed, maybe it would have to do.

Her fingers travelled upwards, feeling the tension in his arms.

'Lindsey,' he groaned softly as she looked at him through her lashes, 'do you have any idea what you're doing to me?'

'I'm not sure I do,' she murmured as her fingers traced the sensuous mouth. 'I never seem to be able to think straight when I'm with you. Shall I stop?'

Niall groaned. 'I'd better warn you that I'm not sure I can.' Slowly he dealt with the buttons of her shirt, and she gasped as his fingers caressed the soft swell of her breasts. 'Have you any idea how much I want you? I can't let you go, you do know that?'

'I'm not sure what I feel, except that. . .'

'You can't deny you want it too?'

'I never felt this way before,' Lindsey whispered.

'But you want me?'

'Yes,' she sighed. 'Yes!' How could she deny it when her own body was betraying her? A shudder of desire racked her. 'I love you.'

She felt Niall tense and stared at him bemused, uncomprehending. She wasn't even aware of having spoken the words aloud until she saw his face tauten with some undefinable emotion as he held her from him.

She said hoarsely, 'Niall. . .' Suddenly her throat was tight; a pressure seemed to be constricting her lungs, making it difficult to breathe as a tiny alarm bell began to ring in her brain. He had said he wanted her. . . needed her. Not once had he mentioned love.

His voice was very controlled. 'You must believe I didn't want this to happen.'

She stared at him, shakily struggling to draw the buttons of her shirt together.

'It's Claire, isn't it?' Niall didn't need to answer. His shocked expression said it all as she pulled away. 'Of course, I should have realised.'

'What the hell are you saying?' Suddenly there was anger in his voice. 'Claire has nothing to do with this. She means nothing to me. She's no longer a part of my life.'

Lindsey choked back a cry of disbelief as she scrambled unsteadily to her feet. 'How can you say that? You don't even believe what you're saying!'

'Lindsey. . .'

'No!' She drew a shuddering breath, backing away as he made a move towards her. 'You're using me as some sort of buffer between yourself and your feelings for Claire. But don't you see?' she pleaded desperately. 'It won't work. Making love to me may help you to forget for a while, but it won't change the feelings you obviously still have for her, whether you care to admit it or not.'

A nerve pulsed in his jaw. 'Can you seriously doubt what we have between us?'

Lindsey shook her head. That last kiss had been a mistake, an aberration. Colour swept her cheeks at the memory of it. She couldn't imagine how she had allowed it to happen when everything within her head warned against it. But it was all the proof she needed of her own vulnerability where he was concerned. He swept her resistance aside as if it were a cobweb. Well, she wouldn't be caught out again.

Lindsey swallowed hard. 'I realise she hurt you, but I won't be used simply so that you can get back at the world. I won't be a substitute!'

'You don't know what you're saying.' His voice was low and even. 'What I feel for you is different.'

Yes, of course it was. He had *loved* Claire. Deep down he still loved her.

'I'd like to go back now,' she said harshly. Tears burned at the back of her eyelids, but she daren't let him see. It would simply give him one more weapon to use against her.

She moved away, heard him call out after her. But she ignored it, the desire to escape overriding all other emotions.

She had made a fool of herself. Maybe, if she could have accepted him on his terms. . . But she knew now that she couldn't. For her there could be no half-measures. Loving Niall, she wanted. . .needed. . .a total commitment in return, and that, it seemed, was the one thing he wasn't prepared to give.

CHAPTER ELEVEN

IN THE days that followed, each one taking the ship closer to home, Lindsey knew she had never been more glad of the solid routine which, if it didn't keep her mind fully occupied, at least kept her hands busy. And as long as she worked, she told herself, she would survive.

There was an odd, almost frightening unreality about everything. Where Niall was concerned, by means of careful avoidance, she hadn't seen him, other than at a distance, for the past two days. On a ship the size of the *Ocean Empress* it was surprisingly easy, especially when it seemed he was adopting the same principle. She should be grateful that he was making things easier than they might otherwise have been. Yet, perversely, she still found herself looking for him.

'There we are, Mr Robertson!' Lindsey smiled sympathetically as she handed over a prescription. 'These tablets should help to get rid of the migraine. They act quickly, and you'll also find they help to ease the queasy tummy, which is a bonus.'

Mr Robertson smiled weakly as he rose to his feet. 'I don't know how it happened,' he sighed. 'I haven't had an attack like this for a couple of years. I thought I'd actually got rid of the damned things. It would have to happen now, wouldn't it?'

Lindsey smiled as she also rose to her feet. 'Funnily enough, that may be the clue. Research shows that diet is a very strong contributory factor to migraine. Certain foods can trigger an attack. It may be chocolate, oranges, cheese, any number of things.'

He laughed wryly and winced. 'That's the trouble with a holiday like this — too many temptations!'

'You'll be fine,' Lindsey laughed with him. 'If you can sleep for a couple of hours, while the tablets take effect, I'm sure by this evening you'll feel much more your old self.'

She was seeing him out when Jill appeared, smiling and attractive in her white dress. 'Nice timing! I'm just off for a coffee. Are you coming?'

'Oh, I wish I could!' Lindsey glanced hesitantly at her desk. 'I'm dying for one!' Along with a couple of aspirins, she thought, briefly kneading the throbbing at her temple. 'I'm going to have to clear some of this first, though. I've got a report to finish. Niall left a note specifically asking for it.'

'Have you seen him this morning?' asked Jill.

'No, why?' Lindsey busied herself rearranging a pile of magazines.

'Oh, no reason. Just that he's seemed a bit out of sorts this past few days.' Jill shrugged. 'It's probably nothing. End of a trip coming up, all the usual hassles.' She deposited a set of keys on the desk and straightened up, grinning. 'And you and I won't be part of it.'

'You really don't mind, do you?' queried Lindsey.

'Funnily enough, now that it's actually here, I can't say I do. In fact, if I'm really honest, I'm quite looking forward to doing something different.' Jill's eyes sparkled. 'I've been offered a temporary job at a private clinic. Tony's joining a big communications outfit, and it's all working out pretty well.' Her gaze rose shrewdly to her friend's face. 'How about you? Niall muttered something about your going into general practice.'

'I think it's time I put down some roots.' With an effort Lindsey managed a smile. 'I think I might do that better on firm ground.'

'So it looks as if it's the end of the line for both of us.'

'It looks like it.' Lindsey gave a slight smile. 'In the meantime we've still got a couple of days left, and I'd better start getting my act together, or my replacement is going to wonder what sort of service we've been running here! Actually——' she frowned at her watch as she followed the other girl to the door '——I definitely think I'd better give the coffee a miss. I've just remembered I'm due at a meeting in about half an hour.'

'Well, don't work too hard.' Laughing, Jill turned away, and Lindsey was about to close the door when Niall appeared in the corridor.

Her stomach tightened in a sharp spasm of apprehension before she half turned away, intending to close the door, only to find that her movements were frozen. His appearance shocked her. He looked tired and drawn, and for a moment, she told herself there was a look of pleasure in his eyes before it vanished and he reached out to prevent the door closing.

'Lindsey, I need to talk to you.'

'I don't think we have anything to say. . .'

His body stiffened as he watched her. 'Don't worry, Doctor. It's business,' he said drily.

She sighed heavily and took an unsteady step back. 'In that case, you'd better come in. What's the problem?'

'I've just had an urgent radio message from Max Stoner in London.'

Lindsey instantly recognised the name of one of the country's leading consultants, and her eyes widened. 'Why on earth would he want to contact you here?' she wanted to know.

'Because it seems they've managed to come up with a bone marrow donor.'

She stared at him. 'You mean. . .for Anne Hammond?'

Niall nodded, raking a hand through his hair. 'I don't know all the details. It may not be a perfect match, but from what I can gather, it's as near as dammit.'

'Oh, but that's wonderful! When do they want to operate?'

He frowned. 'That's the problem. You've seen for yourself, her condition is deteriorating by the hour. I've given a report to Stoner, based on the latest assessment. It's pretty much what he expected, and it makes the timing more urgent. He said, and I agree, if she doesn't have the transplant within forty-eight hours at the outside, it could be too late.'

Lindsey looked at him. 'Forty-eight hours! But we aren't due to make another port of call before we reach home.'

'I realise that,' said Niall. 'Which is why I've spoken to the captain and put him in the picture. We could make Vigo in about four hours. It's an unscheduled stop, but he's already managed to get clearance. I've also spoken to Medicalert, and they can have a plane standing by, ready to fly the Hammonds direct to London, where an ambulance will be waiting. With a bit of luck and some good timing, she could have the operation within twenty-four hours.'

Lindsey felt the tears of emotion pricking at her eyelids. Instinctively she reached out her hand. It was immediately covered by his. 'It's the miracle they've needed and never dared hope for,' she said quietly.

His mouth tightened. 'There aren't any guarantees. They must know the risks. There's always a chance she may be too weak to withstand the treatment. Her body may reject the bone marrow.'

'Even so, I'm sure they'll want to take that chance. Wouldn't you,' she queried vehemently, 'given the same set of circumstances?'

Niall drew a harsh breath and released her. 'I'll finish making the arrangements. You'd better talk to them, make sure they're ready. We can't afford any delays.'

'There won't be any,' Lindsey gave the quiet assurance, and thought she heard him mutter 'good girl!', but told herself she must have imagined it, as he was already striding down the corridor.

As far as the passengers were concerned, the unscheduled stop and the sight of an ambulance drawn up on the quayside lent an element of excitement to spirits which were beginning to flag slightly as the end of the cruise loomed closer.

As the ship resumed its normal course, Lindsey made her way to her cabin, her mind still buzzing with what had been a well handled and straightforward transfer from ship to shore.

There was an hour yet before she need put in an appearance in the restaurant for the evening meal. She decided to use it, adding a generous amount of her favourite scented oil to the water gushing into the bath before lying back and letting the warm water soothe her weariness and tensions away.

When finally she emerged, having bathed and shampooed her hair, she shook her head, the honeyed strands moving in a silken swath about her face. She should have been feeling relaxed, but too many thoughts still crowded in on her, and there were no solutions to any of them.

Forty-eight hours from now, she thought, staring at her pale reflection in the mirror, Anne Hammond would have been given the miracle of the chance of a new lease of life, while her own future seemed to stretch emptily ahead with nothing but work to fill it.

She had chosen to wear a simple but beautifully styled full-length dress in pale amber crêpe-de-Chine, and because the evenings were decidedly more chilly now as the ship headed north she slipped the matching jacket over her bare shoulders. She was just clipping jewelled studs into her ears when the tannoy system suddenly burst into life and the strident, adrenalin-boosting words filled the ship.

'*Sundowner . . . sundowner. Bermuda Bar. Sundowner. . . Bermuda Bar!*'

It was the emergency signal. Lindsey reacted instinctively. Almost without being aware of it she was running, barefoot, she realised later. Her slender-heeled shoes stood where she had left them.

As she headed for the stairs her mind was already trying to calculate the time since the call. A few seconds, but every one vital in the case of a cardiac arrest.

Up the stairs and through the doors. Ten seconds, maybe. Ten seconds in which someone had stopped breathing. On the third deck she met Jim, also running. Fifteen seconds, twenty. . .

The Bermuda Bar was one of the most popular on board. It was crowded with silent people, voices stilled as they became aware of the drama suddenly being played out in their midst.

'Let me through, please, I'm a doctor.' The ranks parted and, as if by a miracle, Lindsey saw Niall, on his knees, bending over the man spreadeagled face-down on the floor.

'What happened?' She flung herself down beside him.

'He was standing at the bar, having a drink, when he suddenly collapsed.' Niall rolled the man gently over on to his back, ripped open his shirt and placed an ear to his chest. 'I can't get a heartbeat.'

'No pulse, no respiration,' Lindsey confirmed. The man's face was dotted with perspiration, his mouth hung half open, his lips were already pale blue. 'How long has it been?'

'At a guess, almost a minute,' he said grimly. 'He's dead, but not brain-dead. We've got three minutes maximum if we're going to save him.' Clenching his fist, he brought it down hard in the centre of the patient's breastbone. 'Come on, dammit! Breathe!' He repeated the action, waited for the rise and fall of the man's chest. It didn't come. 'I'll try mouth-to-mouth.'

Bending his head, he checked inside the patient's mouth, tilted his head back, took a breath and breathed into the man's mouth.

As he drew back, Lindsey watched as the chest expanded and Niall repeated the procedure again and again. 'Let me try. Conserve your energy.' Shifting forward, she placed her hands down firmly on the sternum, forcing oxygen into his lungs. 'One. . .two. . . three. . .four!' With a quick sigh of relief she saw Jill and other members of the emergency resuscitation team beginning to arrive breathlessly on the scene.

'Let me take over there.' Jim dropped down beside Lindsey, taking over the cardiac massage.

They were all aware of the stark tension around them. 'Does he have a wife, any relatives on board?' Niall queried grimly. 'We need some background information, medical history, anything.'

'His wife's gone to the cinema,' someone said.

'Get her here, fast! Try not to panic her. We need to know if he's taking any medication.'

'How long?' Jill asked quietly.

'Two minutes.'

The patient had at least some colour now. His skin had taken on a more normal pink tinge, but there was still no heartbeat.

One. . .two. . .three. . .four. . . Then Niall took over again, breathing precious air into the man's lungs.

Lindsey was aware of Kerry Foster, the senior theatre sister, leading a quietly sobbing woman into the bar. She rose to her feet, going quickly towards them.

'What is it? What's happening?'

'It's your husband—I'm afraid he's poorly. We need to know his name,' Lindsey said calmly. 'Anything you can tell us.'

'It's Tom—his name's Tom Dawson. He's going to be all right?'

'Is he taking any medication?' Lindsey persisted gently. 'We need to know. Was he being treated for any medical condition?'

'No, nothing.' The woman stared at her wide-eyed.

'He can't be ill! He's never ill. We've been married nearly forty years. He hardly ever has a cold. . .'

Lindsey signalled to the other girl to take over. 'We're doing everything possible, Mrs Dawson. Your husband collapsed, we don't know why. . .'

'He's not going to die. He can't die! What will I do?' sobbed the wife.

Lindsey had to turn away. The wires from the cardiograph machine were attached to Tom Dawson's chest. 'He's fibrillating.'

'Defibrillator.' Jill had already handed the gel-smeared paddles to Niall. 'Everybody stand back.' He placed them firmly on the man's chest and pressed the buttons. Tom Dawson's body arched and jerked.

Lindsey stared at the cardiograph, willing it to monitor a response. 'Nothing.'

'Stand clear,' Niall said again. 'Defibrillator, two hundred joules.' Again the man jerked and stiffened. Still no response. 'Keep on with the resuscitation.'

'Get a catheter into a vein.'

Jill slipped the needle in. 'Dextrose in. Five per cent.'

Niall fed a suction tube into the patient's mouth. 'Let's have an endotracheal tube.' He introduced it into the throat, past the vocal cords into the trachea. The oxygen bottle was attached.

'Adrenalin,' Lindsey murmured. 'Five milligrams.' The needle was in her hands. 'Right, flush.'

'What's the history?' Niall glanced up at her.

She shook her head. 'Nothing.'

'Hell! Right, let's stop the massage and see what happens.'

'He's still fibrillating.'

The paddles were applied again. 'Stand clear.'

'Lignocaine. Adrenalin. Dammit, why isn't he responding?' muttered Niall. 'Defibrillate.'

Suddenly Lindsey felt her own heart give a slight jolt. She stared at the graph. 'We've got a pulse!'

There was an audible gasp of tension. This time there was definitely a response. Tom Dawson's heart was beating, irregularly at first, but then, gradually, it became even and steady.

'We've done it! He's going to be all right!' There were unashamed tears in Lindsey's eyes as she sat back on her heels, staring into Niall's sweat-filmed face.

He brushed the back of his hand against his brow, the corners of his mouth flickered, then cracked into a grin. 'I should bloody well think so!' His hand reached out to press hers, then he was straightening up, wearily stretching his back. 'Let's get him to the hospital. Lindsey——' he caught at her arm as she made to move away '—well done!'

She nodded, blinking hard. Suddenly the lack of sleep and tension seemed to be catching up in one great wave of dizziness.

I'm going to faint, she thought incredulously, then became aware of Niall, his hand suddenly firmly beneath her elbow, propelling her into the cool darkness, out on deck.

'Take deep breaths,' he ordered.

What did he think she was doing? It just didn't seem to be having any effect.

'We almost lost him,' she whispered.

'Almost,' his voice reasoned as he came to a halt, shaking her slightly as he turned her to face him. 'But we didn't. It was close, but he's alive, and that's what matters.'

He was right, of course he was. So why was she reacting like this? She should have been ecstatic. Instead of which she found herself having to blink away the sting of tears that blurred her vision.

Tom Dawson had hovered on the brink between life and death, and all the time they had worked so desperately to save him, she had been aware that it wasn't just one life they had been fighting for but two.

'They'd been married for nearly forty years, did you know that?' she said in a small voice. 'Can you imagine what it must be like to lose someone who's been part of your life for so long?' Far worse never to have known that kind of love, an inner voice seemed to say.

'Don't.' Niall's fingers brushed against her mouth, silencing the words. She shivered, though whether from shock or the deepening chill of the night air, she had no way of knowing. In an instant Niall had removed his jacket, placing it round her shoulders. It felt nice, like a shield, it seemed to draw her into its warmth.

She closed her eyes briefly, savouring the scent of him.

'Lindsey?' He made no attempt to release her. Instead, his arm tightened round her as he drew her towards him.

The shock of his touch seemed to rob her of what little control she still had, and her eyes flew open, her blurred gaze registering his gaunt face as she stared at him before his arms enveloped her.

'Oh, Niall!' she whispered.

His hands tenderly brushed the strands of hair from her face. 'We have to talk. Somewhere along the way we seem to have got a lot of wires crossed.'

She nodded, breathing shallowly.

'It's going to be all right, Lindsey,' he said in a low voice. Then his hands were cupping her face and before she could argue or gather her wits, he had taken her startled mouth with his own.

The kiss took her breath away. 'Lindsey — oh, Lindsey, if you knew how much I've wanted to do that! These past two days have been hell.'

'For me, too,' she said brokenly.

Niall gazed wonderingly into her eyes, then, almost hesitantly, enfolded her again in his arms. 'I was afraid if I saw you I wouldn't be able to keep my hands off you. I wanted to carry you off to bed and make love to you.'

'So what stopped you?' she asked breathlessly, her senses still deeply disorientated by that kiss.

He drew her to him, his blue eyes searching her face intently. 'Do you know what you're saying?'

She whispered, 'I was never more certain of anything in my life. Since I met you things have never been the same, I realise now. I never felt this way about anyone.' She had to force herself to speak through the tightness in her throat. 'Maybe it was seeing the Dawsons that made me realise that you can't lose something you never had.' Her voice broke. 'I suppose what I'm trying to say is that. . . I understand how deeply you've been hurt, must still be hurting, but. . .' She tried to look away, but he wouldn't let her. 'I love you. I always have and always will, and we seem to have wasted so much time.'

A groan rose from deep in his throat. His arms tightened round her as though he couldn't bear to let her go and he kissed her again, hungrily.

'I hear what you're saying, but you're wrong,' he

said. 'I meant it when I said that Claire no longer figured in my life.'

'But. . .'

'Don't you realise, there could never be room for anyone but you. Yes, Claire walked out on me and on our marriage. But it was over long before that,' he insisted flatly. 'In the beginning, like an idiot, I chased after her. . .'

Lindsey made a small explosive sound. 'You mean it happened before?'

'Claire liked the idea of marriage. Marriage to a doctor held an even greater fascination. Unfortunately the novelty soon wore off.' Niall grimaced. 'After a while I stopped blaming myself and simply accepted the fact that it was nothing personal, no major failing on my part, it was simply the way Claire was. Then you walked into my life, and I suddenly realised that what I had felt for Claire may have been sexual attraction, but it was never love.'

Lindsey looked at him, her eyes very wide. 'But you made it perfectly clear that you disapproved of ship-board romances. I thought. . .'

His mouth touched hers, tenderly possessive. 'You thought I was pining for Claire?' He gave a soft, rumbling laugh. 'I *don't* approve of shipboard romances. I do happen to have responsibility for nearly two thousand lives on board, though God knows my powers of concentration have been tested to the full of late.' He gazed down at her, his eyes incredibly blue, glittering with the desire. 'But I don't make the mistake of confusing a brief holiday fling with the real thing.' His voice roughened. 'I've wanted you, loved you, since the moment you walked into that room with your eyes blazing, ready to do battle. But I didn't feel I had the right to ask anyone to share the kind of life I lead.'

'It wasn't your fault. Claire knew what the job involved. If she'd loved you, she would have wanted to make it work.' Lindsey drew a long, shaky breath. 'Say it again.'

He frowned, then laughed softly. 'You're not planning to do battle now? If so, I give you fair warning, this time I'll play dirty if I have to. I'll do anything to keep you in my arms.'

She moved closer, teasing him with the softness of her body against his taut maleness. 'Say you love me.'

'I love you. I want you so much,' he whispered. With a hoarse groan he bent his head to the soft curve of her breasts, kissing the smooth valley. 'We've wasted so much time.'

She whispered softly, 'But no more.'

His kiss moved to her eyes, her ears, her throat. 'I can't let you go. I need you with me.'

'You won't have to,' she told him.

His mouth ceased its feverish searching as he raised his head to look at her. 'But the job. . .your uncle. . .'

'It wasn't a definite offer,' she confessed huskily, laughing as his mouth found hers again, taking revenge in a kiss that took her breath away.

When finally he released her she drew a long breath and mumbled inarticulately into his shirt front, 'I don't know what's wrong with me. I'm usually perfectly rational, yet suddenly I seem to be doing things I've never done before.' She tilted her head back to look at him. 'I think I really must be in love.'

'That's a dangerous diagnosis.' Niall looked at her, his mouth slanted.

Her breath snagged in her throat as he stroked her hair, his mouth brushed her forehead. 'What's the prognosis?' she smiled.

'Once you've got it you're stuck with it.'

'Oh, well, that's fine,' she sighed stoically, 'I think I can live with that,' letting her fingers drift idly beneath his shirt.

'Be careful, woman,' he growled. 'You don't know what you're letting yourself in for.'

'So show me,' she murmured, her gaze meeting his with glittering anticipation.

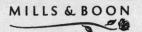

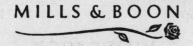

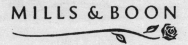